☆·STELLA·ETC.·☆

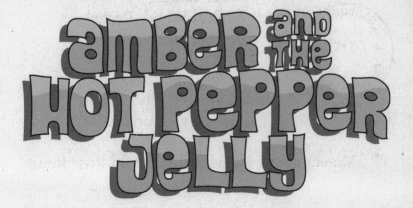

AMBER AND THE HOT PEPPER JELLY

WITHDRAWN
FROM STOCK

KAREN McCOMBIE

For Wendy
(writer, mother, Peruvian explorer)

Scholastic Children's Books,
Euston House, 24 Eversholt Street,
London NW1 1DB, UK
A division of Scholastic Ltd
London ~ New York ~ Toronto ~ Sydney ~ Auckland
Mexico City ~ New Delhi ~ Hong Kong

Published in the UK by Scholastic Ltd, 2005

Copyright © Karen McCombie, 2005
Cover illustration copyright© Spike Gerrell, 2005

10 digit ISBN 0 439 97348 1
13 digit ISBN 978 0439 97348 9

Printed and bound in Denmark by Nørhaven Paperback A/S, Viborg

2 4 6 8 10 9 7 5 3

The right of Karen McCombie to be identified as the author and of this
work has been asserted by him in accordance with the Copyright, Designs
and Patents Act, 1988.

Papers used are made from wood grown in sustainable forests.

CONTENTS

1: How to un-dull a day   3

2: Who needs kneecaps?   14

3: Turning detective (OK, *eavesdropping*, then. . .)   27

4: Eccentric, freaky, whatever. . .   36

5: The seagull, the doughnut and the disaster   43

6: "The x72467%$4£ Café"   55

7: Strangeness, shocks and shrubbery   65

8: Hide (and no seek)   80

9: Stranger than strange   89

10: Know your inner dog   102

11: Bright ideas x two   110

12: Amber's big, fat, boy fib   119

13: Megan's truly, madly *mad* idea   136

14: I spy a lie   142

15: "*Ja, ich bin aus*, er, Norfolk. . ."   156

16: The Great Make-*under*   163

17: What-a-phobia?   171

18: Amberella *shall* go to the ball. . .   177

From:	*stella*
To:	Frankie
Subject:	Makeovers and make-unders!
Attachments:	Amber and the hot pepper jelly

Hi Frankie!

You know what a disaster zone my room is, right? (What – you quite liked the torn wallpaper, crumbling plaster and damp stains?! Ha!) Well, the amazing news is that my dad says he's going to do it up next week! Can't believe it. . .

Actually, I *really* can't believe it, since he's only halfway through fixing up the living room, kitchen, dining room and loo downstairs. Mum's going crazy – she's chucked so many throws and nice bits of material over the various messes Dad's been making that the house is starting to look like the fabric department of John Lewis.

But I really hope Dad keeps his promise. . . Now that I'm meeting new friends, it would be great to be able to take them up to my room and not ask them to wear a hardhat in case of falling masonry. OK, so it's not *that* bad, but it's definitely not that good either (by *miles*).

By the way, my room's not the only place that's getting done up next week. That café we went to

1

while you were here – the Shingles – it's getting a bit of a makeover. I don't think Phil the owner would have thought about giving the place a brand new look, except for the fact that *I* vandalized it, with the help of a) a psycho seagull and b) a doughnut. Oops. . .

See the attachment for the full story (plus stuff about the make-*under* that happened too!).
Miss you ☹, but M8s 4eva ☺!

stella

PS Peaches just killed a seagull. Luckily, it was made out of balloons. He's trying to look like the *BLAM!* of it exploding didn't scare him, but the fact that the claws of all four of his paws are wedged in my shoulder makes me doubt that a teeny-tiny bit. . .

CHAPTER 1

How to un-dull a day

It was going to be dull, not having clowns for neighbours any more.

"Pity they can't stay for ever," I murmured, as I watched John (aka Mr Mystic Marzipan) wrestle a unicycle, a box of oversized clown shoes and an inflatable pig down the narrow lane between our houses to a waiting van.

"*Yes, but now their work here is done, I guess it's time for them to move on. . .*" TJ growled dramatically, putting on the sort of deep American bloke's voice that's always used for the "coming soon" movies at the cinema. (It was a pretty good impression of a man-size growl, since TJ's a 13-year-old boy, and shorter-than-your-average 13-year-old boy at that.)

My bedroom window was pushed open all the way, and me, TJ and Bob were leaning our elbows on the sill – well, maybe not Bob, since he has no elbows – watching the Mystic Marzipans pack up their trampette, Punch and Judy stall, luminous juggling bats and clown costumes.

It had been very entertaining having them around for the last few weeks, listening to the mad CLANK! CLANK! *ScreeeeeeecchhhHHHH!*, thumpety-thumpety-*thump* and THUDDY-THUDDY-THUD-THUD, *boooooooinnnggg!!!* noises they made as they rehearsed their various acts in the house across the lane.

And during Portbay's Gala last week, it had been fun spotting them down on the prom, frightening small children with balloon dinosaurs, and startling sunbathers by doing somersaults over them before handing them flyers for all the various events going on.

"*Everyone's* leaving this weekend," I murmured some more, feeling as flat as a deflating dinosaur balloon.

I knew I was exaggerating – "everyone" only meant the Mystic Marzipans and Megan. But since I hadn't lived in Portbay very long (four weeks) and was still only just getting to know people, I wasn't exactly crazy about the idea of three of the people I liked a lot disappearing on me.

Specially when one of those people – i.e. Megan – had become part of "Stella Etc.". (By the

4

way, I'm not so big-headed that I gave me and my new mates that name – my Auntie V came up with the whole Stella Etc. thing, 'cause it saved her the hassle of ever having to remember any of my friends' names.) Minus Megan, Stella Etc. was now back to being just me, TJ and Rachel.

"Hey, Stella," said TJ, his gaze still on the inflatable pig that Mr Mystic Marzipan was trying to stuff into the van. "D'you realize that Megan's been gone for. . ."

He went all silent then, but from the way TJ's forehead had crinkled cutely and his lips were moving ever so slightly, you could tell he was thinking. *Hard.*

I had a feeling he was trying to come up with the hours, minutes and seconds since our mate Megan had headed home after her holiday here in Portbay. I also had a feeling that it might take TJ a long time to do that, since he once mentioned something about setting a new school record by failing his last five maths tests in a row.

So, I decided not to rush him. (Just as well Rachel wasn't with us; she'd be tutting, rolling her eyes and making sarky comments about him hurrying up and getting to the point before we all died of old age. . .)

Instead, I carried on watching as Mrs Mystic

Marzipan – otherwise known as Bev – rushed out to help her husband stop the inflatable pig from making its escape and floating off into the warm, blue sky.

Then I reached sideways and scratched Bob on the head (he liked it, he's a dog).

After that, I saved a bit of scratching for my cat Peaches too, as he leapt up from the kitchen roof and joined us on the window sill, eclipsing part of the view with his big, fat, ginger-y furriness.

By the time I'd watched, scratched and manoeuvred Peaches over a little bit, TJ *still* hadn't done his sums, so I thought I might help him out.

"Ages?" I suggested.

"Yeah . . . it feels like Megan's been gone for *ages*," TJ agreed with me, "even though she only left yesterday morning. Weird, that, isn't it? The whole time thing?"

The whole time thing was *seriously* weird all round. My old life in north London felt like it happened in another galaxy, not just something I left behind at the beginning of the summer holidays. I mean, I really missed Frankie and the rest of the girls back in Kentish Town, but I couldn't imagine not hanging out on the beach most days with TJ and Rachel (and Bob, of course).

Speaking about the beach, I took in a long,

6

deep lungful of salty sea air . . . and let it out as a huge, never-ending sigh.

"What's up with you today, Stella?" TJ asked, as the never-ending sigh finally ended.

"Dunno. Just feel a bit fed up, I guess."

"How can you feel fed up? We've just had a totally mad week!"

Maybe that was the trouble . . . the past week had been *so* mad (in various good, bad and amazing ways), that I think I was suffering from a large dollop of anti-climax this Sunday morning. I mean, it wasn't *every* week that you meet a new friend (Megan), get roped into a secret holiday romance (between Megan's sister and Rachel's brother), enter a Talent Contest (don't remind me) and watch a disastrous Gala Princess competition (the organizers would *never* live it down). That's not to mention me and my friends turning into local celebrities (kind of), with that story about us and Joseph's house in the *Portbay Journal*.

"Maybe Portbay's just going to seem a lot quieter with no gala and no clowns and no Megan," I said to TJ, telling him the shortened version of what I was thinking.

Honk!! Honk!! Honk!!

"Hey, guys!"

The honking and the shout . . . . it was the Mystic Marzipans, waving us a final farewell from the lane. But it was no ordinary farewell wave – most people don't say bye while honking a red nose and making strange squelching noises (Mr Mystic Marzipan) or balancing on their husband's shoulders juggling purple suede balls (Mrs Mystic Marzipan).

"That's it, then?" I shouted out of the window, shielding my eyes from the sun and hoping I wasn't going to do something dumb like cry. "You're off?"

"Off to entertain a whole new town!" smiled Bev. "But here're a couple of things to remember us by!"

And with that, she delicately tossed the three suede juggling balls one by one over our wall, where they plinged neatly into an old terracotta plant pot.

"For you, TJ – keep practising!"

"Thanks! I will!" said TJ, grinning and giving Bev the thumbs-up.

"And we know you like seagulls, Stella," John called out, stopping with the squelching and sending a white balloon bird sailing and swooping over our garden – and thankfully the assorted prickly weeds – to land by the back door.

What made them think I liked seagulls, I

wondered? I'd never taken much notice of them – except for the psycho seagull that used to stalk TJ. I guess I was kind of fascinated by that particular bird, since it had a habit of lurking, and eating fairy cakes. And I was pretty sure that *The British Book of Birds* (or whatever) didn't list "lurking" and "has a sweet tooth" under its list of traits for the average herring gull.

Still, it didn't look like I was going to get much of a chance to ask Bev and John where they'd got the idea from, since they were on the move. . .

"So long!" they both laughed, as Bev did a forward tumble down to the ground and bounded over to the driver's door of their van.

"Have a great summer!" yelled John, jumping into the passenger side and giving his nose a final honk-honk.

And that wasn't all.

As the van grumbled into life and slowly made to move off, John threw something out of the wound-down van window, high into the air.

The sharp *bang!* was enough for Bob – with a whimper he turned and tried squashing himself under my bed. But me, TJ and Peaches watched transfixed as a chandelier of silver glitter burst in the air and slowly fluttered and twinkled to the ground.

If there were prizes for goodbyes, I reckon Mr and Mrs Marzipan should have won one, *definitely*. And they should have won a prize for cheering me up a bit too. There's nothing like a bit of sparkle – and a daft balloon seagull – to make a girl smile.

"Prrrrp. . ." prrrped Peaches, agreeing with me (I think), and sounding as impressed as a scruffy, fat ginger cat ever can.

"Megan would have loved that!" I laughed, as the last pieces of glitter turned from something spectacular to just some more litter on the pavement.

"Well, text her and tell her!" said TJ. "We promised her we'd stay in touch!"

"Yeah, you're right – we should," I nodded, turning to find my mobile in the clutter of my room. "Oh, TJ – look!"

I guess it was simple maths – even simple enough for a boy like TJ who'd failed five maths tests in a row. Basically, one huge, hairy dog into one tiny space under the bed does *not* go.

Poor pooch . . . while we'd been admiring the sky-show send-off courtesy of the Mystic Marzipans, a stressed-out Bob had improvised and done the next best disappearing act he could come up with.

"Aren't ostriches meant to do that?" said TJ,

tilting his head as he gazed at the bit of Bob that he could see (which was quite a lot).

"What, shove their heads under duvets?" I grinned at TJ. "I don't think you get many duvets on the plains of the Serengeti. . ."

"No, you know what I mean," he grinned back my way. "They just hide their heads and think no one can see the rest of them."

Well, you could see the rest of Bob pretty easily. He looked like a hunched-over brown bear from this angle. And now Peaches had gone and jumped on to the bed, keen to investigate the head-shaped bump under the covers – by, er, squishing his paws into it and settling down on top of it for a snooze. . .

"Hey, Bob – there're no more bangs, boy!" TJ called out to his dopey dog. "You can come out of there now, before Peaches smothers you!"

Bob didn't move a muscle. Not a hair on his very hairy body flickered. The matching grins on our faces started to fade away fast-ish.

"He's not . . . I mean, he hasn't had a heart attack 'cause of that bang or something, has he?" I asked, feeling a flutter of panic now.

(The word I'd avoided using was "dead". Though avoiding using it didn't mean TJ wasn't thinking it too. . .)

"Bob? *Bob?*" said TJ anxiously, hurrying over and hefting Peaches up. Luckily, Peaches' claws were buried in the duvet, so it lifted into the air as well, saving precious time.

For a heart-stopping, hard-staring second, it looked to me – and I'm pretty sure TJ – that Bob really was dead. The way his eyes were closed and his tongue was lolling, it could only mean one terrible thing. . .

And then he let out a long, low, rumbly doggy *snore.*

"*Aaaaaruuuuuffffffffffnnnn!!*"

Good grief – only a dog as dense as Bob could go from absolutely traumatized to fancying a nap in the space of a few seconds.

"Hey . . . let's see how many of your clothes we can pile on him till he wakes up!" TJ suddenly suggested, now that he knew he didn't have a dead dog on his hands.

"I've got a better idea!" I said, rifling in my bottom drawer for the flippers, goggles and swimhat that I knew were in there.

"Brilliant! And have your little brothers got waterwings?"

"Yeah – Jake's got Bob the Builder waterwings and Jamie's got Pingu. Which set do you want?"

"Get both – then there'll be one for each leg!"

12

said TJ. "And grab your camera while you're at it too. Once we get Bob dressed up, we can e-mail the photo to Megan!"

Well, maybe there's no way this next week can be as mad as last week, I thought to myself, *but even the dullest days are bound to be fun if I'm hanging out with an idiot like TJ.*

"Prrrp!"

Was Peaches agreeing with me again? Nah. He'd just spotted a stray silver twinkle of glitter breeze through the window, and was off to pounce on it – but not before giving me a quick green-eyed wink. (The fat furry weirdo.)

"Hey – I just had another idea!" said TJ suddenly. "Quick, get Rachel on the phone!"

Just like I'd hoped, TJ was all set to un-dull the day. Brilliant!

Wonder what stupidness he had in mind. . .?

Chapter 2

Who needs kneecaps?

Two weeks ago, Rachel had had her first ever epileptic fit. (No fun.)

Pretty quickly, she had her second epileptic fit. (*Double* no fun.)

Touch wood there'd been nothing else since.

Well, there *had* been a few of those weird turns she takes, where she can hear things that aren't there, see things that are hidden from view, and know what people are about to say.

That all sounds very spooky and special (and it *is* spooky and special, like when she "knew" where to find the old gold locket buried in the sand over by Joseph's house). But as she says herself, this new gift of hers isn't *always* spooky and special. Sometimes it's spooky and sort of, well, *useless*. Like when she knows that an ad for toilet cleaner is coming on TV right after the ad for Herbal Essences, for example. Or when she knows the exact second her brother Si is about to blast his

14

thrash metal music on/ask to borrow money off her dad/belch.

And right now it looked like she knew everything her mum was going to say. But maybe there were no special powers at work this time; maybe Rach knew instinctively what was coming next because it was the *exact* same conversation her mum had been having with her for the last two weeks.

"Now, if—"

"—I feel even just a little bit ill, I'll call you *straight* away," Rachel wearily finished her mum's sentence.

"Because—"

"—you'll drop everything and come and get me in the car. Yeah, yeah, I know."

"And please make sure—"

"—I eat properly, and don't get too tired. Could you just *leave* now, Mum?"

"What's she *like*?" Mrs Riley laughed in mine and TJ's direction, brushing off her daughter's blatant rudeness.

I grinned awkwardly back. I still couldn't get used to the way Rachel spoke to her mother, but then again, I'd been around them both enough to hear her mum come out with some real clangers (chatting loudly about her daughter's periods in a

15

crowded hospital waiting room didn't exactly thrill Rachel, I remembered). Mrs Riley was just one of those brash, confident women who meant well but tended to stick their foot right in it. In a *very* loud voice.

"Well, have a lovely day, doing . . . whatever it is you're all going to be doing!" Mrs Riley beamed at us, pausing for a second, hoping someone might tell her. But in solidarity with Rachel, TJ and I just smiled silently back at her.

The short silence was finally broken by Bob panting, as he frantically scratched-scratched-scratched a back paw in search of a flea tap-dancing in his hairy shoulder blade.

"Bye, Mum!" said Rachel, a forced grin fixed on her face.

"Bye, darling!" said Mrs Riley, finally getting back into her car. "And don't forget, if you—"

"—feel weird in *any* way at all . . . yes, I'll call! Oh, please, please, *please* go and give me a break for a little while!"

The first sentence was said loudly, the second was hissed softly, between Rachel's teeth, with the fixed grin still in place.

As Mrs Riley drove off along the High Street into the steady stream of daytrippers' cars headed for the beach, Rachel waved like a dutiful daughter.

"Don't move, you two," she said a little louder, talking again through her grin, without her lips moving (she'd make a great ventriloquist). "Don't give my mum the *slightest* clue about where we're going or what we're doing. I feel like I'm permanently under surveillance. . . By the way, where *are* we going and what *are* we doing today?"

For the last part of *that* sentence, Rachel dropped her grin – i.e. as soon as her mum's car had turned left along the prom and slipped safely out of sight. Instantly, her face reverted back to its natural very pretty/slightly sulky look (imagine a Siamese cat with long brown hair and strawberry lip-balm and you've got her).

"Dunno," TJ answered her with a shrug. "Hanging out, mostly. But first, we're going in *there* – all of us together!"

He pointed at the photo-booth outside Woolworths.

"That? That's the 'hurry-up-and-meet-me-and-Stella, we're-going-to-do-something-really-cool' thing you phoned me about?" Rachel said, with a frown of disbelief. "What's so wow about that? We've done it before!"

"OK, so TJ probably made it sound more wow than it is," I said, jumping to TJ's defence. "But it's a fun idea: we all squidge in and get some dumb pics of ourselves – with this sign – then I can post them to Megan in the morning!"

The "sign" was a piece of white cardboard with "Hi Megan!" scribbled on it in black marker.

"Whatever. But I didn't really need anything wow to get me out of the house today, *trust* me," said Rachel, pulling a pink comb out of her minuscule pink leather bag and smoothing her already smooth hair in the mirror on the side of the photo-booth. "Mum's been wittering on to me all morning about keeping a journal of my moods, in case they trigger my fits; my brother's still sulking over what happened with Megan's sister; and on top of that, my dad just announced he's watching Sky Sports all day and we just have to lump it."

"The journal's a good idea, maybe. . ." I suggested.

"Oh, yeah, *right*," said Rachel, shooting me an are-you-*crazy*? look. "And of course, my mum would *never* dream of looking in it, would she?"

"I guess she would. . ." I winced, seeing what Rachel meant.

(I could also see once again in my head that vision of the bouncy castle deflating, revealing Si and Megan's sister Naomi snogging madly, with a half-drunk bottle of cider by their side. Oops!

That had gone down *really* well with Megan and Naomi's parents, I *don't* think. . .)

"Never mind all that, Rach," said TJ. "Why are you bugged about your dad watching Sky Sports all day? Haven't you got a TV and Sky in your own room too? I thought you were spoilt rotten!"

"Oi, you!" Rachel gasped, lashing a lazy swipe at TJ for his cheekiness.

"Aaaaaaaaaaaaaarrrfffffffff. . ." grumbled Bob, muscling protectively in front of TJ and letting Rachel know any swiping of his beloved master was *way* out of line.

"TJ?" squeaked Rachel nervously. "Get him off me!"

"He's not *on* you, Rachel! And Bob – chill out, she didn't mean anything!" said TJ, ruffling the fur on his dog's head to reassure him. (For a second it looked like TJ was about to reach up and ruffle Rachel's hair too, but he wisely decided against it. Her bite was probably worse than Bob's. . .)

OK, it was up to me to sort the situation out.

"Look, everyone just squash into the booth and let's get on with it – I'm going to put the money in . . . *NOW*!"

That did the trick. Sort of.

CLICK!

"You held the sign up too high, Stella – it won't

be in the photo!" TJ moaned, making a grab for the piece of cardboard.

"Well, *you* hold it then!"

And TJ did, lunging sideways so that he nearly knocked me off the stool.

CLICK!

"TJ! You leant too far over! The message won't be in the photo *again*!" moaned Rachel, who was for some bizarre reason kneeling at our feet, sharing the minuscule space with a panting Bob.

"*You* hold it then, if you're so clever, Rachel!" TJ answered, squishing his bum on half the stool next to mine. "What are you doing sitting on the floor anyway?"

"I don't want to be in the pictures – my hair's not sitting right."

CLICK!

There was nothing wrong with Rachel's perfectly perfect hair (of course), but there *was* something wrong with the way she was holding up the sign – it was upside down.

"Look, we've only got one more photo left," I pointed out, whirling the piece of card the right way up. "So let's do it proper—"

I didn't get to "—ly".

And the reason I didn't get to "—ly" was because I fell off my seat when a small ginger something slithered his fat furry self into the booth with a "prrrrrp". Luckily for Megan, TJ had the presence of mind to hold up both Peaches and the scribbled-on card to the camera, so that I would be able to send her the most amazingly brilliant snap in the morning.

CLICK!

"Hey, puss – did you follow me down here or something?" I frowned at Peaches, scooping him up into a cuddle and half-tumbling out of the booth. (Who could help tumbling when there was a big hairy dog and a scrunched-up pretty girl on the tiny bit of floor in front of you?)

Peaches didn't answer me, which was no surprise, I guess, since he's a cat. All he *did* do was rub his furry face against mine, so that a whole bunch of hairs stuck to my nose and cheeks and eyes. At the first sneeze, he was off, leaping out of my arms.

"Peaches?" I called out, temporarily blinded by the itching hairiness and the fact that I'd rubbed my eyeballs fuzzy with my knuckles.

"Omigod, TJ," I heard Rachel moan in the meantime, "why does your dog *always* have to lick me?"

"It's his way of showing he likes you."

"Yeah, well, tell him thanks, but I really *hate*

smelling like a bowl of rancid pet food," I heard Rachel grumble.

She was probably rubbing dog drool off her face with a tissue right now. And the reason I could only guess what she might be doing was, 'cause I was still having trouble focussing. Blinking hard, all I could make out was a few shadowy shapes further along the pavement, with not one but *two* bright splodges of ginger in view.

"Yap! Yap! Yap!" two very small shadowy shapes suddenly yapped.

The frantic blinking finally helped me focus, *just* in time to see Peaches skip elegantly (well, as elegantly as a fat cat can) past the two preened shih-tzu dogs currently straining on their leads after him. And then he was gone, meandering down a side street to wherever his wanders took him. Which left me staring (while TJ and Rachel happily bickered and Bob happily panted) at the other blur of gingerness that I'd made out: the red head of Amber, the miseryguts waitress from the Shingles café. She must have been on her way there now – she was dressed in her usual uniform of baggy black dress and white apron, and perma-scowl.

"Yap! Yap! Yap!"

"Felix! Oscar! Be quiet!" said a small woman

standing with Amber, holding the two straining leads tightly.

The small woman telling the dogs to shut up was Amber's mum. Not that they looked anything alike. Noseying at the two of them together, it was a bit like someone pointing to a bee and an anteater and expecting you to believe they were related. OK, so not many bees are small and dainty with hive-shaped big blonde hair, and not many anteaters are tall and skinny with scruffy red pigtails, but you get the idea.

"Now *that* . . . that is just *gorgeous*," cooed Amber's mum, turning her attention away from the shih-tzus to a shop window. "That would be *perfect* for you for Saturday, Amber. I'll meet you on your lunch-break tomorrow and we can come here and see how it looks on you. How about that?"

From where we were standing, I couldn't see what Amber's mum was cooing over, but the expression on Amber's face – which seemed to say "please kill me now" – made my stomach go squelch with sympathy.

"Mum, if I wore that, I'd look like I was going to a fancy dress party as a *freak*," Amber groaned, her face flushed a vivid pink that clashed badly with her red hair.

"Don't be silly, darling, you'd look just . . .

lovely!" her mum replied, though she seemed to be struggling to find the right flattering adjective.

"No I wouldn't," said Amber, crossing her skinny arms defensively against her flat-ish chest. "Anyway, there's no point even looking at it, 'cause I can't go on Saturday. Phil says I can't get the day off."

"*What?*" gasped Amber's mum. "What are you talking about? You told Phil about Saturday months ago, didn't— Oh my *goodness*! No, no, NO! Shooo, doggy, *shooo*!!"

"Yap! Yap! Yap!"

Uh-oh. While TJ and Rachel had been having fun winding each other up and I'd been earwigging on the nearby conversation, a bored Bob had decided to find himself something to do. And that something to do appeared to be sniffing the bottoms of the two shih-tzus. The shih-tzus weren't very happy about it and were currently yapping, snarling and twisting themselves in a knot around Amber's mum's legs and tottery high heels.

"Bob!" TJ suddenly called out. "C'mere!! *Now!*"

"What's that stupid dog up to?" laughed Rachel.

"He's only trying to be friendly," I said, as we

watched TJ pat his thighs and try to encourage Bob to come back to him.

"Yeah, well, that's my mum's friend Sandra and she's *very* fussy about who's friendly with her little fancy show-dogs!" Rachel explained. "Bob's probably a bit too much of a slob for. . . Oh, he's not about to do what I *think* he's going to do, is he?"

But Bob was currently doing *exactly* what Rachel thought he was going to do – positioning himself beside Amber's mum, lifting his leg and weeing against the shop window.

"Bob! I said c'mere, *NOW!*" yelled TJ, as the pool of wee spread out across the pavement, nicely soaking Amber's mum's tottery high heels as she struggled – and failed – to move away in time, thanks to the leads wrapped round her calves.

I could think of only one thing to say.

"*Run!!*" I yelled, turning and zooming off along the High Street.

I could hear Rachel giggling and panting for breath behind me, and Bob – thrilled that something now seemed to be happening – shot past in a furry blur.

Not sure if TJ was keeping up with us (well, his legs were that bit shorter), I quickly glanced over my shoulder. And there he was, thundering along the pavement in his Converse baseball boots, his T-shirt flapping in the breeze and his skinny tummy on show to the world.

Just for a millisecond, I spotted another thing on show to the world . . . a grin. As her mum gasped and flapped and tried desperately to untangle herself, Amber stood grinning after us and I could hardly believe the transformation. She looked like a totally different girl from—

"STELLA!!" yelled Rachel.

I guess running and looking backwards at the same time isn't a great idea. It just makes it difficult to notice oncoming litter bins.

Hey, who needs kneecaps anyway. . .?

CHAPTER 3

Turning detective (OK, *eavesdropping*, then. . .)

"Oh. Oh, *no*," mumbled Mum.

It was Monday morning and Mum, me and my twin baby monsters – Jake and Jamie, aged two-and-a-bit – were on the High Street.

Unlike yesterday (when only a few tourists were mooching about, plus me and my mates, and Amber and her mum), today was busy with locals shopping for whatever it was that they were busy shopping for.

"That poor girl!" Mum muttered some more, staring into a shop window.

"Dat poo girl! Hee hee hee!" giggled Jake.

"Dat poo. Poo. POO!" Jamie giggled louder.

Ignoring my muppety brothers (always the best thing to do) I nodded in agreement with Mum. The shop window we were looking in was the one Amber had been stuck in front of yesterday, and although I had no idea which of the "lovely" outfits her mother had been trying to talk her into, it was plain to see that every dress in the window of Barbara's Boutique was seriously nasty. Yet seriously expensive too. (Good grief; what kind of person would pay bucketloads to look bad?)

"They're all so. . ."

". . .disgusting," I finished Mum's sentence for her.

"I *was* going to be tactful and say shiny and pastel. But you're right, Stella, they *are* disgusting. And they're also way too middle-aged for a young girl of . . . how old did you say Amber was?"

"I'm sure TJ said she's a couple of years above him at school, so that would make her fifteen."

"Hmm. I wonder what she was supposed to get all dressed up for on Saturday?" Mum mused, still pulling a face at the over-priced, under-styled frock horrors.

"Didn't manage to hear that much," I told her. In fact, I'd told Mum everything that had happened yesterday afternoon – Bob's weeing episode included. Well, I couldn't exactly hobble home with two bruised kneecaps and say I had no idea how they got like that. Plus, my mum is pretty groovy (which comes from spending years working in the marketing department of a very hip magazine in London, I suppose), and I knew she'd be sympathetic when I explained how traumatized Amber looked at her mum's styling suggestions.

"Stella, I know we've had our disagreements," said Mum, tucking her dark hair behind her ears, "but I promise you one thing: if I ever try to make you wear anything like this, you have my permission to sack me as your parent."

That made me smile. We *had* had our disagreements, me and Mum – and Dad, of course. Over stuff like moving here to Portbay in the first place and leaving all my best friends behind. Like being made to swap a great room in a great flat for a bedroom that looked half-built in the DIY disaster zone that was our new (very old) house. Like banning me from exploring inside Joseph's house in Sugar Bay any more, in case I put my foot through a rotten floorboard or had the crumbly roof fall on my head or something.

The first two points didn't matter any more (I'd grown to really like Portbay and I'd put up enough posters in my room to cover the plaster cracks, torn wallpaper, etc, till Dad got round to fixing it up, whenever *that* might be). The last point still hurt though – I'd come to love the ancient mansion and everything I'd discovered there, bit by mysterious bit. . .

BLEEP!

"Is it from Frankie?" Mum asked, as I quickly fished my mobile out of my pocket.

For a fleeting second, I realized something: Frankie, not to mention Parminder and Eleni and Neisha and Lauren – none of them were texting or phoning or e-mailing as often as they had when I first left them behind in London.

But there was no point moping over that when I had a text message to answer. . .

"No – it's from Megan," I said to Mum, automatically following her along as she began steering the double buggy of noisy boys away from the horror of Barbara's Boutique towards our next port of call a few doors further on.

Got yr e-mail last night. Can't believe we've got matching purple knees! M x

It took a second to get what Megan was on about – and then my mind re-wound to last Thursday, when she'd cartwheeled across an empty town square and slap-banged herself into a lamp post.

Well, *there* was a coincidence (the knees, I mean). But hey, I was getting used to them (coincidences, not knees). Somehow life in

Portbay was full of coincidences, and luckily – or spookily – enough, Peaches my cat had a funny habit of pointing a few of them out to me with a fat furry paw or a wink of a green eye. Actually, I had a feeling that him turning up in the photobooth yesterday was a coincidence too; one with some kind of hidden meaning. I just had to work out what the heck the hidden meaning was. . .

Oh, and speaking of coincidences, there was another one now, ambling along on the other side of the road and turning into the alley that led to The Vault, Portbay's cool CD and vintage comic shop. The name of this particular coincidence was Simon Riley (i.e. Rachel's brother) and he must have been on his way to his summer job at The Vault – late, it looked like. Still, it must take quite a while to put that black eyeliner on, and get the whole disaffected I've-just-thrown-this-whole-grunge-thing-together look just right.

By the way, I might've sounded like I was slagging Si and his style but even if I wasn't wild about the eyeliner or the pierced lip or the T-shirt with the rabbit's skull on it, Si Riley *did* happen to be devastatingly gorgeous to look at.

Just seen Si, I texted back to Megan, as I followed Mum and the buggy into Bailey the

Butcher's. *Rach says he's still moping over yr sis.*

Mum was ticking off things on her shopping list and the boys were singing a song they'd just made up about poo, so while I waited for Megan to get back to me, I idly started listening into a conversation the smiley butcher was having with some woman as he hacked a defenceless hunk of meat to bits.

". . .oh, yes, the wife and the girls are all in a complete tizz about my niece's wedding on Saturday. You know what you women are like about dressing up! Well, maybe not my youngest . . . she's not so much into clothes. And she's not really the sort to get in a tizz about anything much. . ."

His customer blah-blahed something in reply that I couldn't make out.

"Oh, yes! The two oldest are both doing great! April's *loving* her college course and Ashleigh's working alongside her mum in the salon. A couple of stars! And they've both got crackers of young lads – couldn't have picked better for 'em myself!"

Whack!, went the sharp, shiny big blade, slicing another chunk of meat in half. (*Wow*, how brave must a boy be to date a butcher's daughter. . .)

The customer blah-blahed something else,

which must have been a question from the way her voice lilted at the end of the sentence.

"My youngest? She hasn't really got any ambitions, I don't think. Or any boyfriends on the horizon, come to that!" the butcher said jovially. "Bless 'er, she's not quite in the same league as her sisters!"

Y'know, I felt like I was listening to one of TJ's mum's amateur dramatic productions of *Cinderella*. The two indulged, petted older sisters, the dowdy, ignored baby of the family.

Poor girl, I thought to myself, wondering who Portbay's Cinders was exactly.

Poor girl. Hey . . . that's what Mum had said about Amber two minutes ago. And what were Amber's sisters called again? Yep – they were Ashleigh and April, and this man had just mentioned a family wedding happening on Saturday. A family wedding that everyone would have to be dressed up for, of course!

Without wanting to sound like some corny detective, it all suddenly made sense. . .

BLEEP! went my mobile.

Naomi's moping 2. Wot u up 2? Megan had tap-tapped to me.

I was thinking about what to write back (*Hanging out in butcher's*, wouldn't sound too exciting) when the butcher's booming voice grabbed my attention again. Only this time, he wasn't chatting about poor old Amberella. . .

"Really? Started boarding up the windows this morning, did they?"

Whack! Whack!

"Well, better to be on the safe side. I mean, I know this campaign to raise money to save the chandelier is all very nice, but you can't have holidaymakers' kiddies wandering in there and hurting themselves. The sooner the old place is demolished the better, *I* say."

Whack!

That last whack wasn't the sound of meat being dissected – it was the sound of my heart thundering against my ribcage, as I realized the butcher was talking about Joseph's house.

The council were boarding up the windows? It would be like *blinding* the place. It felt like a worse kind of vandalism than the stone-throwing and smashing that Portbay's "friendly" local thug Sam and his braindead mates had done recently.

My first instinct was to run over to Sugar Bay and see what was happening with my own eyes.

And that's exactly what I would've done, if it

34

wasn't for the tiny matter of being banned from going anywhere near it.

I couldn't get round that little problem, could I?

Could I. . .?

CHAPTER 4

Eccentric, freaky, whatever...

There was no getting away from it: Mum and Dad had banned me from going to Joseph's house.

So I wasn't at Joseph's house. Er, technically speaking...

Well, put it this way: my parents had banned me from *going* to Joseph's house, but they hadn't banned me from *looking* at it. Which is why I was now at the caravan park perched high on the headland, between bustling Portbay beach and the normally deserted Sugar Bay.

There was no road to Sugar Bay – just a rubbly steep set of steps that wound down from the caravan park. Not that any of the tourists staying in the Sea View Holiday Park ever seemed to venture down there (guess that was 'cause it was a deckchair/chips/ice-cream free zone). Apart from the seagulls, the only living creatures I'd ever seen on the sands or exploring the old house in the last few weeks were a) my friends, b) Sam's gang, who'd come to vandalize it, and c) the police, to arrest Sam's gang.

"Toffee?"

It might be a very sweet, little word, but my first instinct was to jump.

I was jumpy for two reasons: first, because it's pretty normal to jump when someone you hadn't noticed speaks loudly in your ear all of a sudden, and secondly, because I'd told Mum a tiny white lie so I could come here. ("Megan texting again?" she'd asked, barely glancing up from her shopping list in the butcher's. "Er, no," I'd fibbed to her. "It's TJ. Can I go hang out with him?" "Of course!" Mum had smiled, not realizing her daughter was a bare-faced white liar with pants very much on fire.)

"Oh . . . hello!" I said, turning to see Mrs Sticky Toffee standing smiling right beside me.

"Eccentric", that's what my Auntie V would call Mrs S-T. And Auntie V knows an eccentric person when she sees one, since she's an actors' agent and says they're *all* pretty eccentric. "Freaky" is what my friend Frankie would call her, since Frankie is quite good at being blunt.

Both of them had been to Portbay but just on quick visits, so neither of them had met the eccentric, freaky Mrs S-T.

"Um, yes, thank you," I muttered, as Mrs S-T lived up to the nickname I'd given her and held out a bag of rustly wrapped toffees. This close up, I got a good view of the peachy, old lady face-powder she must've patted neatly on her old lady face this morning. The netting on her neat pink hat wibble-wobbled in the light summery wind.

"Well, I bet *they* were saying a few swear-words!" said Mrs S-T, unwrapping a sweet for herself and popping it in her mouth.

As usual, I hadn't a clue what mad Mrs S-T was on about.

"Er . . . sorry? *Who's* swearing?"

"Those men from the council," Mrs S-T replied, nodding at the men up ladders, hammer-hammering boards across the top windows of the house, now that they'd finished the job on the downstairs ones. "They can't have had much fun having to leave their van parked up here and carrying all their equipment down there."

"Don't suppose so," I said, finding myself smiling a little bit, sort of glad at the idea of the men having a hard time of it. It was like Joseph's house wasn't giving in easily, or something. (Or maybe I was just a little bit completely *mad* for thinking that four walls and a roof could fight back.)

"You're a bit of an artist, aren't you, dear? You should come up here and draw the old place, before it's gone for good."

Mrs S-T . . . we'd run into each other plenty of times since I'd arrived in Portbay, and she always managed to speak in confusing circles or rambling riddles or whatever and completely confuse me. But what she'd just said – about coming here with my pad and drawing the house before it disappeared was the most clear and simple and true thing she'd ever said to me.

"Yeah . . . I will," I nodded, wondering if I could stand white-lying to my mum again.

"I'm sure Miss Grainger and Joseph would be thrilled if you did."

My heart lurched at the mention of the young girl who once upon a time lived in the house, and the young black boy who'd been her servant – and best friend.

"If there were such a thing as ghosts, of course," Mrs S-T chuckled. "Jam sandwich?"

See what I mean about her? She could send shivers shooting up your spine and then offer you a snack in the same sentence.

"Thanks . . . but I'm not hungry."

"Oh, it's not for you, dear – it's for him! Couldn't get my hands on any fairy cakes today!"

39

Before I got the chance to say anything, Mrs S-T had pulled a sticky sandwich out of her shiny cream handbag and shoved it into my hand, at the same time as pointing at the slightly cross-eyed seagull hovering in front of us on a cross-wind.

He's looking fat, I thought, as I dutifully tore the bread and threw it into the air for the sweet-toothed psycho seagull to catch. *He should be eating fish, not fairy cakes and jam sandwiches. Maybe he'll be the world's first obese seagull. I could put him in for the* Guinness Book of Records. . .

"Isn't that your phone, dear?" Mrs S-T mentioned, fidgeting with the stubborn clasp on her bag.

"No, I don't think so," I said, just as the phone began to trill.

Weird. It was like Rachel knowing stuff right before it happened. What was it with this town? Everyone was born with the weird gene, *that's* what.

"Stella? It's me," TJ yelled in my ear, above the sound of his kid sister singing "Under The Sea" in the background and Bob howling along. "Fancy meeting in the Shingles for a milkshake or something? I've got to get out of the flat or I'll go mad – Ellie's watching *The Little Mermaid* for the fifth time in a row. . ."

40

"Yeah, OK. I'm not far from yours – I'll come by your flat."

"Why – where are you?"

"Um, Sugar Bay."

"But aren't you, well, a bit banned from there?"

"Long story. Tell you later. Bye!"

There's nothing worse than being reminded you're a liar. (I guess death, starvation and torture are worse, if you're going to get nit-picky, but at least they don't make you blush till you're beetroot.)

"Off to meet your friends?" Mrs S-T smiled.

"Mmm," I nodded, throwing the last hunk of sandwich into the air (nice catch, psycho seagull).

"Ah, how lovely to have friends. And she's a lovely girl. . ."

"Who? Rachel?"

I was frowning. I liked Rachel a lot, but that was in spite of her coming across as a spoilt, sulky princess. I couldn't see how Mrs S-T could describe her from looks alone as "lovely".

"No, that's not her. I mean . . . now what's her name again? Dear me, I'm always forgetting things these days. Her name . . . it matches her hair – does that make sense?"

I'm not like my old friend Frankie, I'm not very good at being blunt. But right at that second, there was only one answer I could think of.

"No."

And with that, I scuttled off, waving a bye over my shoulder at Mrs S-T as her apple-green raincoat flapped in the breeze and the obese psycho seagull flapped fatly just above her. . .

CHAPTER 5

The seagull, the doughnut and the disaster

"Old, pink, green and mad."

Rachel had just asked me to describe Mrs Sticky Toffee, and that was the first thing I'd come up with. Old because she was, er, old; pink, because of her meringue hat; green, 'cause of her apple-coloured raincoat and mad, because she most definitely was.

"Nah. Don't know her."

"Me neither." TJ shook his head, his chin resting in his hands, his elbows leaning on the plastic of the café table.

"But you *have* to have seen her going about – she's always feeding the seagull that used to stalk you, TJ!"

"Stella, have you looked around Portbay recently?" Rachel's voice was a cross between little girlish (it was high, with a hint of a lisp), and at the same time wildly sarky. "There are about a zillion old people in this town and about five teenagers. I don't think me or TJ are going to notice one more pensioner strolling along eating ice-cream and tutting about what 'young people' are like these days."

Rachel had been hanging out at The Portbay Galleria, her mum's shop, when I'd called her five minutes ago and said we were in the café, if she fancied coming along. As she'd only been reluctantly dusting horrible (and expensive) ornaments at the time, her answer had been "Yes, please – see you in two seconds."

And while we'd been sitting here waiting for our order to come, I'd told TJ and Rachel about what I'd heard at the butcher's shop (I'd had to whisper it, since Amber was within serving distance of us). I'd also told them about what was going on down at Sugar Bay (though it was frustrating that they didn't know – or particularly care – who Mrs S-T was).

"Is that *hurting* Phil?" Ellie suddenly asked, frowning out of the plate glass window at the owner of the Shingles café.

"Oof! Urgh! Uhhhh . . . *oops*!"

On the other side of the glass from us, Phil was groaning loudly as he struggled to open the faded

44

stripy awning with a metal hook on the end of a big long wooden pole.

"Nah . . . it's just that the awning is really ancient and stiff to yank free, I think," TJ reassured his little sister.

Tugging at the shade was definitely the reason Phil was "oof"ing and "urgh"ing. But the reason he was "uhhh . . . *oops*"ing was called Bob. TJ's mega-dog kept getting up and galumphing around, trying to get out of Phil's way, and naturally getting right in it. The "uhhh . . . *oops*!" was Phil trying to keep his balance after tripping over Bob for about the sixteenth time.

"Maybe we should bring Bob in here?!" Ellie suggested, all bright-eyed and blonde-haired, as she leant over in her chair and pressed her hands and nose up against the window.

"Ellie, you know dogs aren't allowed!"

At her big brother's words, Ellie crossed her arms, pouted and tried very hard to force tears to come to her eyes.

"Whatever, I wish Phil would hurry up and get that shade thing down – the sun's so hot streaming in here!" moaned Rachel, looking like an older version of Ellie, with crossed arms and a pout to match (no tears in her eyes, though it was hard to see since she had her sunglasses on).

45

"There you go: one tea, one orange juice, two raspberry milkshakes and four doughnuts," mumbled a grumpy voice, as the cup, glasses and plates were plonked roughly down on the table.

"Um, thanks!" I said warmly, hoping for a repeat of that grin I'd seen beaming from Amber's face yesterday, when Bob had helped tangle her mother up in doggy knots.

But there was no grin – just the usual downcast eyes and smile-free face.

With the tray now empty, Amber shoved it under her arm and hurried off to her next customer – milky drips dribbling unnoticed down her uniform – pausing only briefly to trip over a folded down kiddy buggy on the way. That got a few stifled sniggers from Rachel's brother Si and his mates, whose table she was hurrying over to serve next. Between a bossy mum, a tactless dad, general humiliation and dribbles, I felt a huge wave of sympathy for Amber.

Still, it was a pity she'd managed to drip some of those milky dribbles down *my* leg while she was at it.

And a pity she'd got our order just a *teensy* bit completely wrong.

"Hey, I know we're all meant to be feeling sorry for Amber right now," muttered Rachel, lowering her shades and staring at the tea she hadn't ordered. "But d'you think we could call her back and get her to bring us the stuff we actually *wanted*?"

"Aw, don't go giving her a hard time. Specially not in front of Phil – you don't want to get her sacked from her summer job!" said TJ, lowering his voice as the bell on the café door pinged and Phil strode back inside.

"He looks *sad*. . ." mumbled Ellie, in between gulps of her orange-that-should-have-been-apple juice.

"Who, *Phil*?!" I asked her, slightly confused.

"Yeah, he's probably sad because he's got the worst waitress in the world working for him," Rachel jumped in. "I mean, do these *look* like muffins?"

She held up one of the sugary doughnuts as evidence.

"I meant *Bob*," Ellie answered my question, already nibbling on her own doughnut. "*Can't* he come in? We could hide him under the table!"

Hiding a dog of Bob's large hairiness under the table? That'd be like keeping a sheep in your sock drawer and expecting your mum not to notice.

"Ellie, for the billionth time, Bob *can't* come in

47

here," TJ sighed wearily. "And Rachel, for your information, Amber is OK."

"Not as a waitress, she isn't. . ." muttered Rachel, not letting it lie. "She's grumpy, she's clumsy, and she gets it wrong."

Rachel had a point. Amber *was* grumpy, and clumsy (having her once drop a plate of cold pasta on my head wasn't exactly fun). And yeah, maybe I should've been stirring my straw in banana milkshake instead of raspberry. But I felt I had to remind Rachel of something, something kind of important.

"What about the night you were singing karaoke in here, Rach? Amber helped you get revenge on Kayleigh and that lot, remember?"

The revenge-by-chillies had been TJ's idea – to sneak extra hot chilli peppers into Rachel's friends-turned-enemies' nachos. Kayleigh, Brooke and Hazel had all given Rachel a hard time since her first seizure, and after chumming up with the morons known as Sam and his gang, they'd got a whole lot worse. So yeah, TJ had come up with the idea, but if Amber hadn't gone along with it and put those stinging nachos under their noses, Rachel might have had a terrible time with hecklers instead of the cheers and applause she'd ended up getting from everyone in here that evening.

48

"Amber didn't do that 'cause of me, or 'cause our mums are friends or anything," Rachel shrugged, "she did it 'cause TJ paid her, didn't you?"

"I offered to, but she left the money on the table."

"Yeah, *right*. She just forgot it, you mean," snorted Rach.

Rachel . . . she'd spent so long working on being selfish and shallow when she was friends with Kayleigh and co that sometimes she blanked the fact that there are times when people do nice things just because they *can*.

"Haven't you ever hung out with Amber, because of your mums being friends and everything?"

Rachel opened her mouth at my question and I could sense a sarky "as *if*!" coming on. But just as quickly she shut it, knowing that she'd promised me and TJ that she'd be a new, improved, non-nasty version of herself if she wanted to stay friends with us.

"Look, it's just that she's a bit. . ." Rachel struggled to find a kinder way of saying what was on her mind, ". . . a bit . . . of a *nerd*."

Oops, she failed.

"Amber's not a *nerd*!" TJ laughed.

"What's a 'nerd'?" asked Ellie, but no one answered. (TJ and Rachel were too busy bickering and I was too busy listening in.)

"No?" said Rachel, flashing her almond eyes at TJ. "Well, how come she sometimes hangs out with that nerdy crew at school, then!"

"Because they're probably the only people in her year who don't tease her!" said TJ, with hamster cheeks of doughnut.

"What do people tease her about?" I asked him, though I was pretty sure I might be able to guess.

"Um, stuff like being so tall and skinny, and blushing all the time."

Yep, I'd guessed.

"And about her name being ginger, the same as her hair . . . stuff like that," TJ went on. "It's a real shame, 'cause she's pretty interesting, underneath, when you get talking to her."

"Amber? *Interesting*?" Rachel said, a little too loudly. "I don't believe *that*!"

"Yeah, well, a lot of people might not believe that you're nice underneath either!"

That was exactly the sort of cheeky remark you'd expect TJ to make. Which was why it was shocking (in a good way) to realize that I'd said it; shocking for Rachel, TJ and *me* especially.

"Hey . . . if *those* doggies are allowed in here,

50

why does Bob have to stay outside?" Ellie moaned suddenly, ignoring what we were wittering on about.

Still jangling from my sudden burst of mouthiness (wow – my London buddies would *never* believe that shy little Stella was getting positively non-shy these days!), it took a second to register what Ellie was going on about.

"Philip! A word, please!" the small, blonde woman bellowed, as she trotted across the tiled floor in her high heels, her prissy little dogs trotting neatly behind her.

"Mrs Bailey! What can I do for you?"

"Well, you can tell me why you want to ruin my niece's wedding this weekend for a start!"

Phil's a big bloke, with a wide smile and a (very) wide waistline that shows he enjoys the food in his café too much. But big bloke or not, he seemed nervous of the small, fierce tornado of a woman who'd steamed in.

"Mrs Bailey, I'm afraid I don't get—"

"Let me spell it out for you, Phil," said the blonde tornado. "It's my niece Jenny's wedding on Saturday and a *long* time ago, Amber asked you for the day off. Only now, you've gone and told her she can't take it off after all!"

The expression on Phil's face reminded me of

Bob when TJ's just told him off and all he's heard is "blah blah blah".

"Hey, Amber!" Phil suddenly turned and called out, glancing over at his pink-faced waitress, who was frozen to the spot in embarrassment, her order pad clutched in her knuckle-whitened hands. "You want to come and translate? I haven't a clue what your mum's on about!"

"She didn't ever ask for the day off, did she?" Rachel muttered.

"Don't think so," I whispered back, realizing two things at once.

1) Now I'd got a glimpse of what her family was like, I guessed Amber had been looking for a way out of going to the wedding for a long time.

2) What TJ had just said, about Amber's name and her hair colour . . . Mrs S-T had meant *her* when she was talking about my "friend"!

Well, right now, the friend I didn't know I had was bolting past the tables and out through the café door, the order pad still clutched in her hands. Every single face in the place turned to watch her escape, and every single one of us saw her trip and go *splat* over a snoozing Bob. To give her credit, she was up and off again in a flash.

Then *zoom* . . . I leapt up from my seat and ran out of the café door too. I don't know why I felt like I had to follow her – maybe it was 'cause my head was still reeling at the idea that mad Mrs S-T had somehow got it right. But I didn't get very far – after only jogging the length of a few of the seafront shops, Amber had dashed off into the distance on her long, deer legs. There was nothing to do but turn back.

"Is he all right?" I called in concern, when I spotted TJ, Rachel and Ellie huddled around a sprawled-out Bob outside the Shingles.

"Yeah – he wants his tummy tickled so he must be fine!" TJ called back to me.

"What were you doing chasing after Amber?" asked Rachel, staring at me through her sunglasses. "Were you going to ask for her to swap *that* for a muffin after all?"

I looked down and realized I was still clutching my doughnut.

"No," I said, smiling at Rachel's sarky joke. "I just felt sorry for her. Wanted to check she wasn't about to have a heart attack with the embarrassment and everything."

Out of the corner of my eye, I saw the stripy café-awning wobble. It was the psycho seagull, landing as gracefully as a sack of potatoes on a jelly.

"He's looking kind of tubby, isn't he?" TJ commented, glancing up.

"He sure is!" I laughed, tearing off a chunk of jam doughnut and throwing it up to his waiting, open beak. "D'you think Weight Watchers take birds? Maybe we should enrol him or some—"

Thruuuunnnnnnnngggggggg. . .

DOINGGGG!!

Scrrreeeeeeeeeeech!

Fizzzzzz-fitz-fizzzzzzzzzzzzzzle. . .

Those were the noises of the awning coming away from the wall, the awning falling in slow-motion towards the pavement, the awning pulling the neon "Shingle Café" sign off the wall above it as it fell, and the neon sign spitting and hissing electricity in a very frightening way.

And all because I'd fed a fat seagull the one chunk of food that tipped his weight over the edge (of the awning).

As the seagull flapped slowly into the air, and my friends and Bob scrambled out of the way, I could think of only one thing: doing a runner, just like yesterday.

If Portbay ever entered the Olympics, I could win the sprint for them, no problem.

Well, there was *one* problem: I'd never be able to show my face in Portbay ever again. . .

CHAPTER 6

"The x72467%$4£ Café"

"Prrrrp!" prrrrped Peaches.

I thought he might be saying "hello", or "thank you for letting me sleep on your chest all night and squeezing the very breath from your body". But no . . . he was prrrping in the direction of the door. Seemed like this "prrrp" meant "You're being watched, check it out."

"Hey, Sleeping Beauty!" Mum smiled from the doorway. "I kept peeking in at you but you were zonked. The amount of hours you've slept, you'd think you'd run a marathon yesterday!"

I smiled back weakly and said nothing. I *had* sprinted back home from the seafront in record-breaking time (shame and guilt really help put a spring in your step).

When I'd got home, I'd been all set to spill out what had happened with the doughnut, the seagull and accidentally wrecking the café. But then I saw Mum leaning on Dad's shoulder as he ate his lunchtime sandwich and read out some report in the *Guardian* on youth crime-waves in urban areas, and decided to keep my mouth shut in case they thought I was a youth crime-wave all on my own.

"Anyway, Stella, you've had three phone messages while you've been having a lie-in."

Three? That must be one from Phil the café owner saying I'd be thirty-three by the time I'd paid him back for the damage I'd done; one from the police telling me to pack my toothbrush as they were on their way round to arrest me and one from the *Guardian* wondering if I'd be interviewed for their next feature on young criminals.

"The first one was from Megan, just saying hi," Mum began to tell me. "The second one was from TJ – he's at the café now and wants you to meet him there as soon as you can, apparently."

Meet him at the café? Was TJ *crazy*? I could never go near the café, or the promenade, or the beach in this lifetime! In fact, I might have to persuade my parents to move again. To somewhere rural and remote, where Phil could never find me. Like Bulgaria, maybe. . .

"And the third one was from the Portbay Museum. They wondered if you could pop in sometime and let them see the photos you took inside Joseph's house, plus the locket you and the others found in Sugar Bay. Sounds like that story in the newspaper got them thinking!"

"Wow. . ." I mumbled, forgetting all the other horrors and guilt for a second.

"Oh, and I forgot," Mum suddenly added. "TJ said to tell you that everything's brilliant, and Phil says you can have a free Coke on him. Does that make sense?"

"Mmmm!" I muttered non-committally, while a voice inside my head yelled "Er . . . *no!*"

Maybe it's like the Childcatcher in Chitty Chitty Bang Bang*!* Megan texted me twenty minutes later, as I warily made my way down towards the seafront. (TJ's mobile was permanently engaged, which is why I'd texted Megan for reassurance as I headed to the café to meet him and my doom. Not that Megan was doing a very good job of reassuring me so far. . .)

What do u mean? I texted her back.

The Childcatcher lured kids with lollipops, then locked them away in the castle. Maybe Phil is tempting u with free Coke, and then he'll pull a lever + you'll end up in cellar 4ever. Ha ha!

It didn't feel too *ha ha* to me, so I switched my mobile off, took a deep breath, and turned the corner from the High Street on to the promenade. And then I saw a familiar sight – Bob sprawled on the pavement like a living, breathing rug. Only he wasn't so much parked outside the café as *next* to it. That's 'cause two blokes were up two ladders, gingerly dismantling the wrecked shop-awning and sign.

Suddenly I was so nervous that I felt my stammer coming back, which was mad, really, since I wasn't even speaking.

I was just on the point of turning round and walking my trainers straight back home again when I saw TJ come out of the caff with a bowl of water for Bob.

"Stell! Stella!" he yelled, spotting me too.

Drat.

"C'mere! It's all cool! Honest!" he yelled some more. "It's better than cool – it's pretty exciting!"

OK, so call me a mug; Phil could be holding Ellie hostage, forcing TJ to act casual and lure me inside with fake smiles and promises. But whatever . . . I decided to risk it. (By the way, I've made myself sound very brave there. What really happened was that TJ came running over before I got it together enough to bolt, grabbed my hand, and dragged me under a ladder and into the café.)

"What's going on? I couldn't get through on

your phone!" I protested, as I felt the tiles under my feet and the smell of coffee, cake, and beans and sausages waft up my nose.

"After I spoke to your mum, Ellie asked to look at my mobile and promised to be careful."

"So?" I said, glancing nervously around for signs of an irate Phil or any strange levers as TJ plonked me down at a table.

"So she instantly dropped it in her apple pie and custard."

"It was an oops. . ." muttered a shamefaced Ellie, blinking her blue eyes hard and nursing a sickly, sticky mobile in a pile of serviettes.

"Whatever," I said quickly, since I was in a bit of a nervy panic. "How can everything be cool, TJ? When you called me yesterday, you told me the fire engine had been here when you left!"

"Yeah, but I came in here this morning to see what had happened and found out there wasn't an *actual* fire or anything. It was just a precaution, Phil said!"

"OK, I suppose. . ." I said, feeling not particularly reassured. "But doesn't Phil want to kill me anyway?"

A large pair of hands chose that second to rest themselves on my shoulders. Uh-oh. . . Phil was going to pick me up like a bag of rubbish and toss me into the back of a waiting police van outside. Probably.

"Why would I want to kill one of my regular customers?" Phil boomed cheerfully, letting go of my tensed muscles and moving round to grin at me. "TJ told me you think it's your fault, Stella, but that old awning must have been getting ready to fall off at any time. I mean, come *on* – how could a doughnut and a bird be to blame?!"

Hey, had he *seen* the size of the psycho seagull? It was like having a pot-bellied pterodactyl land on a buttercup and expecting the little flower to stay standing.

"Anyway, however it might have happened, it's done me a favour."

"Hnmmm?" I squeaked, completely thrown.

"'Oh, scuse me, Stella," said Phil, looking all of a sudden distracted. "I've got to serve those customers – we're a bit shorthanded without Amber. . ."

Seemed like I wasn't the only one to dread showing my face around here after yesterday.

"So what exactly is going on?" I asked TJ, dying to know now that I knew I wasn't in danger of imminent death.

"Phil wants to give the café a makeover. Says he always planned to do it, but never got round to it.

Now he's going to give it a new name and tart it up a bit!"

"There's going to be a competition!" Ellie butted in. "You can win a big secret *thing*!"

"A competition to chose a new name for the place," TJ spelt out more clearly. "I think the big secret is that Phil hasn't decided what to give as a prize yet! But anyone can enter – you just have to write your suggestion up there. See?"

TJ pointed to the blackboard that usually had the specials of the day chalked up on it. But instead of "spaghetti carbonara", "double egg, sausage and chips" and "apple pie and custard", there was just a list of possible new café names scrawled on, in lots of different handwriting. Some were OK, some sounded a bit naff, and one sounded a bit dubious. . .

Tea by the Sea
Posh Nosh
The Promenade Café
The Shore Thing
Eat This

"Isn't that last one really rude?" I mumbled, remembering a boy at my last school who liked to say it as he wandered around, acting like he was in a serious hip-hop band from the Bronx, and not in a Kentish Town school playground.

"Actually, yeah. . ." nodded TJ, "and funnily enough, Sam and his gang were just leaving, laughing their heads off when we got here."

"Which one's rude?" said Ellie, suddenly taking too much interest.

"Never mind," I muttered quickly. "Hey, look – that girl Tilda is adding something. . ."

Si Riley's goth/weird mate had got up from the table she'd been sitting at alone and started chalking something in arty handwriting. (It would *have* to be arty; a girl who permanently dresses in a tutu, stripy tights, chunky boots and a leather jacket would *never* write normally like the rest of us.)

"*A Bite. . .*" Rachel murmured along as the words formed.

"*. . .at the Beach!*" Ellie finished off. "That's nice!"

"Yeah, but knowing her, it's probably got some spooky double meaning," said TJ. "You know; the 'bite' bit *could* mean food or it *could* be a vampire thing!"

"What's a vampire?" asked Ellie.

Er, how do you explain a creepy blood-sucking being to a five year old (without giving them nightmares for the next ten years)?

The answer is, you don't.

"Hey!" I said, moving the subject swiftly on. "Why don't we all try thinking of something nice to call the café?"

TJ slapped his hand on the table, making the cutlery jiggle.

"Exactly! Whatever the prize is going to be, let's win it!"

"*I* know! *I've* got one!" squealed Ellie, clapping her hands together.

"Go on, then," I smiled at her. "What is it?"

"'The Nice Café'!"

Hmm. I didn't think we stood much of a chance of winning the secret prize with *that* suggestion. We needed more brain power.

"I'll text Megan, see if she's got any ideas," I said, whipping out my phone. "Oh . . . hold on. The reception's gone funny. I'll nip outside for a sec. . ."

Weaving around the ladders and workmen, I crouched down by the mighty bulk of Bob – well, I might as well give him some pats and attention while I was texting, I figured, as I began my message to Megan.

Because Bob is so huge, I must've been half-hidden from sight, 'cause when Amber came shuffling along the pavement, she didn't seem to notice me. I noticed *her* all right; and she was kitted out in her waitress get-up, all set to come back to work, I guessed.

And then Amber slowed up . . . and ground to a halt. Was she looking at me, watching *her*? No – she was staring at the café frontage and biting her lip. And then she turned and began to run, doing that impression of a deer in an apron she'd done so well yesterday.

Bleep!

An incoming text from Megan made me jump.

Stella, what does "Hey, got any ideas for a new name for x72467%$4£" mean?

Oops.

Maybe it's not such a good idea to keep on texting and accidentally sending messages when you're busy looking the other way. . . .

ChapTeR 7

Strangeness, shocks and shrubbery

What a strange Tuesday. And it was still only a quarter to one.

First, I'd assumed Phil was going kill me for vandalizing his property.

Then I'd discovered that he didn't hate me and was really pretty pleased to have an excuse to re-vamp his café.

Next, I'd spotted Amber trudging towards the café and then suddenly turning and sprinting away from it at high speed.

And now? Well, now I was sitting in the office of the Director of the Portbay Museum, being offered tea and posh biscuits, and not knowing where to put the chewing gum that was lodged in my mouth.

When I'd got here – after saying bye to TJ, Rachel and Ellie, who'd all preferred to stay on the beach sunbathing/helping Bob dig a hole to the centre of the earth – I'd nearly died when the

65

receptionist had ushered me through the door with "Director" on it. For a second in my panic, the person I expected to see sitting in a museum director's chair was either an insanely clever, slightly dusty, hundred-and-twelve-year-old man, or someone who looked like Ross from *Friends*.

Instead, a smiley, plump woman in a floral summer dress was cooing over the loveliness of the locket I'd just handed her, as well as the photos I'd taken – especially the one of the carving on the window sill of the bedroom I thought was probably once Elize Grainger's.

"Elize and Joseph, friends for eternity, 1841," the woman re-read aloud.

That carving: the weekend that Frankie had come to visit, it had inspired us to scratch out our own version of it in the window sill of my little den in the garden at home: *Stella + Frankie, m8s 4eva, 2004.*

"It's a lovely thing to have stumbled upon, Stella. I can't wait for one of our curators to go and see it for themselves – perhaps we'll be able to save it and display it here at the museum. Our very own example of nineteenth-century graffiti!"

I guess that was the director trying to sound all jokey with me, but it's hard to feel jokey in a place like a museum, which is all about interesting but *serious* stuff. And Portbay Museum was full of interesting, serious stuff. Apart from all the regular local bits and historical bobs that every museum seems to have (old Roman coins dropped by careless Romans; ancient stone beer bottles dropped by ancient drunks; antique instruments of torture to punish peasants daring to sneeze in the presence of lords or whatever), Portbay Museum had saved or copied everything from the ballroom of Joseph's house – except for the giant and hard-to-move crystal chandelier.

When Frankie came here with me all those weeks ago, she'd asked *how* exactly they could've copied what was in the old house, if it wasn't there any more. Good question. And the answer was, at some time they'd got their hands on a very grand, very old painting of ten-year-old Elize Grainger and her parents, posing in the ballroom in its heyday. In the background was all the fancy furniture and decoration that people in the 1800s were into. Also in the background (where servants always were in those strange long-ago days) was Joseph. . .

"But how can anyone get in the house now it's all boarded up?" I asked the director woman, shoving my chewing gum out of reach between my teeth and my cheek so I could politely nibble the posh biscuit.

"Oh, we can get in – with a special permission slip from the council. And a hammer of course!" laughed the museum director, trying to be jokey with me again.

I thought about laughing too, but then I might've choked on the biscuit and the hidden chewing gum.

"Anyhow, Stella, just to give you a quick update: since you and your friends did that fantastic piece in the local paper, we've been promised a large cheque from the Gala committee for the Save The Chandelier fund."

"That's good!" I said, gulping down a bit of biscuit, feeling my chest swell with pride.

Pity that the museum director's large chest seemed to flop with a sigh.

"It *is* good – but we need a lot more money very, very quickly to make it possible to move the chandelier before the demolition teams move in in a few weeks. And I'm not going to beat around the bush – I'm not sure it's going to be possible in time. . ."

The museum director blah-blah-blahed on some more after that but I wasn't really listening. All I heard was "I'm not sure it's going to be possible in time" running through my head over and over again, like it was doing just now as I weaved my way through the caravans up on the headland overlooking Sugar Bay.

As the salty air breezed by, I felt so suddenly soaked in misery that I *had* to speak to a friend who understood. It couldn't be TJ, 'cause his mobile was full of custard. It couldn't be Rachel, because her mobile was on answer service when I tried just now. It couldn't be Frankie, as she'd thought Joseph's house was as interesting as a branch of TopShop with the doors locked and the lights out the time she came to look at it with me (and Neisha and my other old London friends had never seen the place).

Of course, the second I saw the sneezy lemony caravan (OK, a caravan that was really called The Sea Anemone), I knew who to talk to (i.e. Megan, who'd stayed in that particular caravan when she was on holiday here). And I owed her a proper phone call anyway, and not just yet another text.

"Stella!! BRILLIANT! Are you OK? Where are you calling from? It doesn't *sound* like a dungeon!!"

Instantly, I realized how much I missed Megan – she was like a human version of Tigger: always bouncy, even in the way she talked.

69

"No – Phil didn't end up chucking me in a secret dungeon under the caff; I'm up at the caravan park. And like I texted you, Phil was really OK. He's all excited about giving the Shingles a makeover."

"Well, I'll keep trying to think of some *BRILLIANT* name for the place so you and TJ and Rachel can enter it and win that competition!"

And then *blam* – as I kept walking, the view swept out before me, down into Sugar Bay. I'd never seen the sun blast down on it quite like that before, like it was a movie set with heaps of giant spotlights trained on it. The old house looked bleached white and practically brand new, as if it was waiting for a sailing ship to bob around the bay and drop off its first inhabitants – the Graingers who'd come all the way from their sugar plantation in Barbados.

"Hey, Stella, are you sure Phil wouldn't like to call it The x72467%$4£ Café after all? I think it's pretty *ACE*, in a nuts way. . ."

It was too awful to think that such an amazing place, with such a story to it (never mind the ghosts I reckoned flitted around it), was going to get squashed like some soggy old cardboard box very soon. OK, so there was nothing anyone could do about that, but what about—

"Stella? Are you still there? TALK TO ME!!!"

"Oh, sorry!" I gasped, realizing my brain had been lost in space for a few seconds. "I was just thinking about the chandelier in Joseph's house. The people at the museum said they might not raise enough money in time to save it. . . Got any ideas of how to get loads of cash quickly?"

"Rob a bank?" Megan suggested.

"Don't think so. Don't fancy the idea of prison food," I grinned, remembering that you could always rely on Megan to be good at being silly, and useless at being serious.

"What about your mum, Stella?"

"What *about* my mum? D'you think she's got tons of money stashed somewhere?"

That was a joke. My parents may both have had fancy-schmancy magazine jobs in London, but they weren't working at the moment while they got the house together, and I knew ('cause I overheard them the other night) that one or both of them was going to have to start earning by the end of the summer or we'd have to sell off one of the twins or something equally drastic. (OK, so I was joking, again. But when Jamie was in one of his annoying biting moods, selling him to a zoo, or at least swapping him for something nice and cute like a baby llama, is kind of tempting. . .)

"No, I mean, you told me your mum used to work in a marketing department, didn't she?"

"Uh-huh," I nodded, sitting down on a conveniently seat-shaped rock.

"*Well* . . . marketing's all about getting people excited about stuff so they buy it, isn't it?"

Was it? I hadn't ever really thought about it. You know what it's like with parents' jobs; unless they're in a rock band or have shares in Disneyland, you don't get particularly thrilled about what they do or ask for any details. It was like Dad; I knew he used to go to work in expensive but trendy suits and do big business deals. But I still sometimes got muddled about whether he was an accountant or a lawyer or whatever.

"So, maybe your mum could come up with a really *great* idea of how to get people excited about saving the chandelier and raising LOADS of money for it!"

I take back what I said in my head about Megan; she wasn't at *all* useless when it came to being serious.

"Hey, St–lla," Megan's voice juddered all of a sudden. "I might cut ou– now, 'cause I'm on a bus an– we're just go– under a br—"

After a couple of seconds of willing Megan to

come back, I gave up, snapping my silver and pink flip-top phone shut and sliding it into my back pocket.

And then I nearly died of shock.

Well, you don't exactly expect to see a lone leg leap out of a bunch of ferny shrubbiness right in front of you and jerk around, do you?

At least it actually wasn't on its own (that would be *way* too weird) and at least I quickly recognized who the jerking leg was attached to.

"A-A-A-Amber?" I s-s-s-stammered, as a figure dressed in a badly fitting waitress uniform sheepishly rose out of the greenery only a couple of metres away from me.

"Sorry – didn't mean to scare you," she said, flushing pinkly. "I just came up here to be by myself. To lie and look at the sky and stuff. But then I heard you on the phone and tried to stay out of sight – till I got cramp in my leg just now."

"Oh."

"Mmm."

After that, we stayed quiet for a second, Amber and me, both basically shy girls waiting for our pink cheeks to un-pink and our hearts to stop racing.

I wanted to start talking, but I wasn't sure I could trust my stammer to have stopped yet.

And where would I start anyway? ("Pretty embarrassing for you in the café yesterday, huh?" or "Did you know that a mad old lady sort of predicted we'd be friends?")

"Bad bruises on your knees," Amber muttered first, hugging her own knobbly knees to her chest.

"I . . . I ran into a litter bin." ("Running away from you and your mum after Bob weed," I *didn't* add.)

"I know. I saw you," said Amber, with the tiniest flicker of the grin I'd spotted on Sunday (er, right before I ran into the litter bin). "You should rub arnica cream on those."

"What's arnica?" I asked, examining my angry purply-blue knees for myself.

"Herbal stuff. The sort of medicine that's been used for centuries."

"Oh yeah, everyone used to use plants and things from nature, didn't they? It's all meant to be better for you than the chemicals we use now, isn't it?"

I couldn't believe I was chit-chatting about things I knew absolutely zilch about when all I *really* wanted to ask Amber was why she'd turned and run this morning, instead of going into work. . .

"Not necessarily," Amber said, her face

regaining some paleness now that the blush was flushing away. "Rich women used to use white face powder made out of lead. It looked nice at first, but lead's poisonous and rotted their faces away. . ."

"Wow. I didn't know that," I mumbled, thinking that was an interesting, if yukky, fact. (Looked like TJ was right, about Amber being interesting underneath, I mean.)

We both went silent again. I didn't know what Amber's reasons might be, but mine was 'cause I was suddenly hit by the fact that she was two years older and *way* smarter than me.

And then Amber spoke first (again).

"Hey, that is *one* fat bird," she murmured.

A-ha. There was the psycho seagull, in all his cross-eyed, big-footed, plump-bellied glory, hovering on a cross-wind and staring straight(ish) at us.

For a nanosecond, I thought about telling Amber what had happened yesterday after she'd legged it (i.e. the gull, the doughnut, the vandalism, the fire engines). But instead of telling her everything, I decided to try asking her just one tiny thing.

"Amber . . . why did you run away from the café today?"

75

Instantly, Amber flopped back into the ferns, semi-out of sight, and went quiet for a second. But only for a second.

"You saw me?" her voice drifted up from the shrubbery.

"Yes."

"Urgh . . . see, my life is just wall-to-wall embarrassment. I'm cringing 'cause only *you* saw me. And the reason I ran away was 'cause I could imagine *all* the staff and the customers staring at me, knowing what happened yesterday. What a cringe *that* would be!"

"Were you scared that Phil would be angry with you?" I asked.

"No . . . Phil's cool. He phoned and said he wanted me to come back."

"He must think a lot of you."

"It's not that; he pays so badly that all the other waitresses leave after about five minutes. I'm the only mug who he can rely on to stay."

Well, I guessed that solved the riddle about why such a clumsy, grouchy waitress kept her job.

"Do you like working there?"

Y'know, I felt a bit stupid talking to a bush, so I decided to join Amber.

"It's OK, and Phil's a laugh," she said, glancing over as I lay down in the ferns next to her. "But I

76

don't like serving grumpy customers too much. Still, as long as I work there, it means I've got a good excuse not to work in my mum's shop."

"You don't fancy working in a hair salon, then?"

"And get even more hassle about 'making myself presentable' than I do already?" Amber laughed dryly. "'Why don't you try a bit of make-up, Amber?', 'What if I put some blonde highlights in?'"

"Don't you get on with your mum, then?"

"Most of the time, I do. But I always get the feeling I'm a disappointment to her, and to Dad."

"How come?"

"Because I'm too tall, too skinny, too quiet and don't look like I belong to the rest of my perfect family."

Hey, join the club. I mean, me, Mum, Dad and the twins were as much a family as anyone, but thanks to distant relatives that had sprinkled a mad mixture of skin and hair colour amongst us, nobody would guess we were related. But I didn't get a chance to say that, since Amber was seriously off on one.

"Anyway *thanks* to my mum, I'm totally mortified at the idea of going back to work, *and* I've got to go to this *stupid* family wedding on Saturday, where *everyone* will be comparing me to my sisters and asking me corny, embarrassing questions like 'Why don't *you* have a boyfriend, Amber?', when what they're *really* thinking is 'How did Sandra and Joe have this little ugly duckling after such cuties as April and Ashleigh?'"

I'd seen Ashleigh and April at the Portbay Gala – they looked like shorter, curvier versions of Barbie.

"That's pretty tough. . ." I tried to mumble sympathetically as the ferns tickled the back of my bruised knees.

"Yeah? And it's not exactly fun when you've got SAD and agoraphobia and dyslexia on top of everything. . ."

I wasn't sure about SAD, but I'd definitely heard of agoraphobia and dyslexia – though I couldn't remember what they were exactly (not good, I was pretty sure). I was just about to ask when—

Mew-mew-mew-mew-mewww!, came a chorus of cats from somewhere in the ferns.

"Oh, God . . . it's Phil," muttered Amber, sitting bolt upright and staring at her mewing phone. "I guess I'd better go, before he really *does* sack me. . ."

As Amber scrambled to her feet and hurried off with a wave, my head whirled with questions.

What were all those weird conditions she'd mentioned?

Was Mrs S-T right, would Amber end up as my friend?

And how did that slowly circling, fat, psycho seagull know that I had a posh biscuit from the museum stashed in my pocket. . .?

ChapTeR 8

Hide (and no seek)

"I'm not here," Mum muttered, slipping through the door of my den and closing it behind her.

"Er . . . you *look* as though you are," I told her, glancing up from the desk and the caricature I was doodling of the psycho seagull. (I'd got a good close look at him earlier, as he'd perched on the rock beside me, happily crunching his posh biscuit.)

"If your dad or your brothers shout and ask if you've seen me, say no."

At the sight of Mum, Peaches arched up into a furry stretch, jumped off the old armchair he'd been snoozing on and weaved his way between my legs so he could flop down in the cool shadiness under the desk. Mum gratefully sank herself down into the vacant chair, sweeping her thick, dark hair off her face. Her olive skin had darkened even more with the sun these last few weeks, I noticed.

"Are you playing hide and seek with Jake and Jamie?" I asked.

"No – I'm just hiding."

"Who from?"

"From Jake and Jamie. I need a break for five minutes, or I might just throw them in the bin along with *this* stuff."

She pointed to her favourite hipster jeans and fitted Gap T-shirt. They both had lots of small, paint-splodged handprints on them, in the same shade of mint-green paint that Dad was using on the bathroom walls.

"How did they get hold of the paint?"

"Stella, you know your brothers; when it comes to doing things they shouldn't, they are *very* talented and resourceful."

Well, I knew that. The twins seemed to be magnetically attracted to anything of mine, and to keep my stuff from being chewed, ripped, mangled and scribbled on, I'd had to be pretty resourceful too. Like putting my posters on the ceiling instead of the walls of my room. Like putting an old cooker guard around the nail varnish and make-up on my dressing table. Like keeping everything I really loved out here in the den where at least I had a bolt, high up on the door, that I could flick shut when I heard loud yells and the patter of tiny feet approaching.

"I see you've been putting more things on your shelves," Mum commented, kicking off her Birkenstocks and curling her feet up underneath her. "It all looks great!"

The shelves had once been home to a zillion dead spiders and rusty tins of nails, just like the rest of the den had been home to broken-down old gardening tools and decades of dust. But now the same shelves were packed with seashells and driftwood, photos and drawings, knick-knacks from London and antique stuff I'd found hidden underneath all the dead spiders and dustballs.

As I gazed at Mum's face scanning the clutter, a small noise from under the desk made my ears prick up.

Bending down, I saw two green eyes staring hard at me.

"Cuh, cuh," Peaches coughed his catty cough at me. Either it was very dusty under there (very possible), or Peaches was trying to get my attention. And knowing what a spooky cat he was, I guessed the *cuh-cuh*s had nothing to do with dust. . .

But as I wasn't very good at reading mad cats' minds, I ignored him and decided to ask Mum about the weirdy medical stuff that Amber had mentioned. (I guess I could've looked them up on the internet . . . if I'd known how to spell them.)

"Mum, I was talking to one of the waitresses from the café today – the young one."

I decided not to mention *where* exactly me and Amber had had this particular conversation – i.e. how close(ish) I'd been to the banned big house.

"Is that the girl who spilt pasta on your head?" she checked, trying to hide a tiny smile twitching at the corner of her mouth as she spoke.

"Um, yeah . . . that one. Amber. Anyway, she mentioned all these conditions she's got."

"What sort of conditions?"

"Dyslexia, and aggro . . . something-phobia. And SAD, I think she said. I know what dyslexia is – that's when it's hard to read, isn't it? But what are the other two?"

"Poor girl!" Mum frowned. "Well, yes – you're sort of right with dyslexia: it's when people get the images of letters jumbled up and find it hard to make sense of them. And SAD stands for Seasonal Affective Disorder – that's when you get depressed if you don't get enough sunlight. And agoraphobia is fear of having panic attacks when you're outside, or in crowded places. Um . . . is Peaches all right?"

83

"Cuh, cuh," Peaches coughed some more under the desk.

"I'll check," I said, dipping my head down to see what His Fat Furriness was up to.

And what he was up to was staring hard at me again, while pinning a glinting piece of shininess to the floor with one paw. The shiny piece of paper . . . it was part of the exploding chandelier of glitter that the Mystic Marzipans had set off when they left on Sunday. As soon as I thought of that, something *else* pinged into my brain. . .

"Mum – the chandelier from Joseph's house!" I blurted out, banging my head on the desk as I sat up.

"What about it?" she asked, wincing at the dull clunk of head on wood.

What Megan had suggested earlier, I hadn't spoken to Mum about that yet. She'd been too busy trying to stop the twins from out-screaming each other when I'd come home this afternoon. It had been impossible to think, never mind talk, above the million-decibel din, which is why I'd sloped out here to the den to draw and chill out and pick ferns out of my hair.

"The woman at the museum today – she said that they probably won't be able to get enough

84

money together in time to save the chandelier in Joseph's house."

"Oh, really? Wow – that would be such a pity, Stella, especially after the publicity you got about it in the local paper."

Mum looked genuinely concerned, and genuinely interested. I suddenly felt a rush of happiness – I had her all to myself, for once. No small boys distracting her by stuffing their teddies in the toilet or pouring fabric conditioner in the DVD player.

"Mum, Megan thought you might be able to think of something. 'Cause you've worked in marketing, I mean. Y'know, come up with some way of, er, marketing the chandelier or whatever. . ."

I wasn't making myself very clear, mainly 'cause I didn't know what I was talking about. All I wanted was for Mum to wave a magic wand and say she had an amazing idea that would earn bucketloads of money in two minutes flat.

"Well, I don't really know what to—"

"*WAAAAAAAAAAAHHHHHHHHH!!!*"

"Louise! Lou, where are you?" Dad's frantic voice called out. "Jamie's jammed a Fimble up his nose!"

"Omigod, what next with those boys?"

85

mumbled Mum in a panic, shoving her sandals back on and bolting for the door.

So much for our nice chat, our mum-and-daughter moment (it really was just a moment, thanks to Jamie and the Fimble).

Bleep!

An incoming text – good, I needed to take my mind off the disappointment of my alone-time with Mum being cut so short.

We're back at café. Coming? TJ.

Y'know, with everything going on today, my brain had sort of *frazzled*. I suddenly felt a huge urge to lie down on the sofa with a packet of crisps in front of an old episode of *Tracey Beaker*. (Though knowing my luck, Jake would've been sick on the sofa and Jamie would've poured all the crisps into the washing machine. Never, *ever* come to my house if you want to relax.)

So my answer to TJ had to be. . .

Can't – too tired. C U 2moz? PS No custard in phone any more?

Bob licked it clean. Yes, C U 2moz – got something great for us to do!

Hmm, interesting. Like I said before, you can always rely on TJ to un-dull a day.

Bleep!

Another message from TJ already? Nope, it was Rachel.

Don't believe TJ – it's not great, it's naff.

So tomorrow, we were going to do something either great or naff. Whichever it was, it was probably going to be fun.

Bleep-bleep-bleep!

A call now? It was all go. . .

"Hello?"

"Stella – it's the weirdest thing."

The voice belonged to Rachel, even though she hadn't bothered to say so.

"*What's* the weirdest thing?"

"Well, I'm sitting here in the café, and I just went into my bag to get my purse and I found this *envelope*. With 'Stella' written on it!"

OK, that sounded pretty weird.

"What's inside it?" I asked her, with flutters of spookiness flitting around in my stomach.

"You want me to open it and see?"

Rachel had already worked out that my answer to that question was "yes" – I could tell by the sound of ripping paper.

"It says: '*Thanks for listening. Willow*'. Huh? What's *that* supposed to mean?"

"Er, I don't know." I shrugged, though no one – except Peaches – could see me. "I mean, it's nice of, er, *Willow* to thank me for listening, but I haven't a clue who he/she/it is. *Or* what I'm supposed to have heard."

"Prrrrrr. . ."

Oh, yeah – Peaches the All-Psychic Cat probably knew but a lot of good that would do me, since he wasn't too fluent in the English language. . .

CHAPTER 9

Stranger than strange

Go past the pirate and take a right at Bob.

TJ's text directions to Pavilion Park weren't as nuts as they might seem.

I'd never been to the park before, but I'd mucked around at the crazy golf course on the road that led out of town, and the park lay just beyond it. So this morning I headed there – high-five-ing the yo-ho-ho-ing robotic pirate who stood at the crazy golf entrance as I went by – and kept my eyes open for Bob.

And there he was: a flopped blob of hairiness up ahead at an entrance in an endless row of wrought-iron railings. From what I could tell from my peek at it, the leafy park beyond the railings looked really pretty, with a big posh old building in the middle (hope it had a café) and amazing views of the sea (it was perched on a headland at the other end of the beach from Sugar Bay).

I'd have to come here with my family

sometime. Only the twins would probably rip the heads off all the roses and then leap *wheee!*ing into the waves below. . .

Anyway, it was Wednesday, and I'd arranged to meet up with my friends in Pavilion Park for the Annual Portbay Dog Show. This was the something "great" that TJ had come up with for us to do today. Rachel might still think it was naff, but she was here too. Bob would have liked to have checked it out, I'm sure, but as he was a common-as-muck pet and not a show-dog, he wasn't allowed in.

"Hello, nice puppy!" said Ellie, reaching up to pat a rhinoceros-sized Rottweiler.

"Ellie, don't touch the doggie," said TJ, as the Rottweiler's owner frowned at the idea of her prize pooch being sullied by some messy, ice-cream wielding kid. "You're not allowed to touch the dogs, remember?"

Ellie put on her best sulky pout and stared at the ground as we moved off.

"*Stupid* dog show," she mumbled. "Can't take Bob in . . . can't pat the puppies. . ."

In between sniggering at over-preened dogs and their paranoid owners, we were talking about this, that and whatever, including stuff like my weird letter from yesterday.

"Maybe it's a joke. Someone taking the mick," suggested TJ.

"Well, maybe . . . except the message isn't really funny enough to be a joke." I shrugged. "I think it's got to have been a mistake, that's all."

"A mistake?" Rachel frowned my way.

"Mmm. Maybe it was meant for another Stella?"

"Oh, right – like I know *lots* of Stellas!" laughed Rachel.

"Well, *I* don't know," I muttered, feeling confused and a little bit spooked. "I mean, all I *do* know is I *definitely* don't know anyone called Willow!"

"Hold on. . . My next-door-neighbour's got a Siamese cat called Willow!" said Rachel, perching her sunglasses on her head.

"Yeah, but a Siamese cat is *hardly* likely to have written a message, stuck it in an envelope with its little paws and smuggled it into your bag when you weren't looking, is it?"

So TJ was right, but in my experience, Portbay was so packed full of interestingly weird weirdos and general freakiness that I wouldn't have been particularly surprised. . .

"TJ, look! Look!" Ellie babbled frantically. "It's the long girl from the café! The one with ginger hair!"

I didn't know if Amber was one of those red-headed people who hated the term "ginger" or not, but I don't think she'd have exactly *loved* to hear herself described as "long".

"It's 'tall', not 'long'," TJ corrected Ellie.

Ellie wasn't listening – she was too busy running across the grassy lawns to see Amber, who was sitting on a deckchair, gazing down blankly at the two shiny fluff-balls at her feet. Out of her baggy, badly fitting waitress uniform, I'd have liked to have said that Amber was transformed – Cinderella-style – but I'd have been lying. It wasn't that she looked terrible; she just looked . . . well . . . *nothing-y*. She'd decked herself out in a shapeless blue sweatshirt, old loose jeans and trainers that were well past their wear-by date. By contrast, her mum's dogs could've just stepped out of a salon. In fact, since Mrs Bailey owned a hairdresser and beauty salon, they probably had. Just imagine little Felix and Oscar being washed and blow-dried, their fur serum'd for extra shine, before Amber's mum added the finishing touch of matching red velvet bows in their hair. I was desperate to check out their paws when we got close up – I half-expected to see their claws all nicely French manicured.

"Hi, Amber!" I called out, to my potential new friend.

"Oh, hi!" said Amber, with a shy smile and a vivid blush of cheeks when she glanced up and saw us.

"Not working today?" I said, before realizing that was a dumb question. (If Amber had been busy serving the wrong orders to hungry customers in the Shingles café, she'd hardly be sitting here in the park minding prissy dogs.)

"No; it's my day off. My mum dragged me here. She said it was to keep her company but it's really 'cause it gives her the chance to go and nosey at the Pavilion while I mind the dogs."

"What's the Pavilion?" I asked.

"It's that," said Amber, using her thumb to point at the grand building in the middle of the park. "It's where my cousin is having her dumb old wedding on Saturday. . ."

At the mention of the wedding, Amber's face suddenly spelt out "gloom" in a big way.

"So. . ." I said, thinking a change of subject might be a good idea. "How did it go yesterday? Was it all right being back at work?"

"I survived." Amber shrugged, looking pretty uncomfortable. "Wasn't much fun being stared at, and I could've done with a pair of earplugs."

"What for?" asked TJ.

"So I couldn't hear when people were sniggering at me."

"They probably weren't sniggering at you," I tried to reassure her, while thinking they probably *were* sniggering at her, 'cause people can be stupid and mean that way, can't they?

Before we got into any more "Yes they were" grumblings from Amber and "No they weren't" fibs from me, Ellie got all gushy and distracted us.

"Aw . . . they're *sooo* pretty," she cooed, bending down on her haunches to get a closer look at the two gleaming piles of well-groomed fur.

The two gleaming piles of well-groomed fur sniffed at Ellie warily.

"Hmm . . . pretty annoying, you mean," Amber grumbled.

"Don't you like dogs?" asked Rachel, her eyes scanning Amber's outfit critically as she spoke. (Rachel was trying *really* hard not to be as shallow and snobby as when she was in her old group of mean-girl friends but it seemed like some habits were still hard to give up.)

"Yeah, I just don't like *these* dogs very much. Shih-tzus are meant to be all friendly and laid-back, but Felix and Oscar have the personalities of bad-tempered wasps."

"*I* think they're nice," Ellie told her, kneeling down in front of them and optimistically ignoring their low growls.

"Wonder what Alsatians are meant to be like?" said TJ, gazing over in the direction of the now faraway gates. "Don't think they're meant to be quite as dopey as Bob."

"Alsatians . . . they're supposed to be intelligent, loyal, obedient, brave and protective," said Amber matter-of-factly.

"Well, one-out-of-five isn't bad. Bob *is* loyal, I s'pose," grinned TJ. "Though if he had to choose between me and a bowl of dog food, I dunno. . ."

"How do you know that stuff? About Alsatians, I mean?" I asked Amber, thinking that she must have a mind like a computer lurking behind those pink cheeks.

"Oh, I just know 'cause *I'm* an Alsatian." Amber shrugged. And then immediately blushed furiously when she realized how crazy that sounded.

"Huh?" TJ frowned at her.

"Um . . . it's just that there's this website I found – you answer all these questions and it tells you what kind of dog you'd be. If you, er, were a dog, I mean. It's just a stupid thing for fun. . ."

Poor Amber's words faded away to an embarrassed mumble.

"Sounds like a laugh!" I told her enthusiastically. "Can you write down the name of the site so I can try it out later?"

Amber gave me a little pleased smile, her blush ebbing away now like (pink) waves on the shore. I was really starting to feel closer to her, after our chat at the caravan park yesterday, and now this.

"I haven't got a pen, but I could text it to you," she said, whipping out her phone and beginning to key something in before I'd even got a chance to tell her my number.

And then her mobile suddenly began mewing, sending the two fluff-balls at her feet into a yapping, frantic frenzy. (Had she deliberately chosen that ringtone to wind them up, I wondered?)

"Yes, Mum, they're fine," Amber muttered into her mobile, turning away from us slightly. "No, no sign of the judges yet. Hmm? No, sign of them either– oh, no here they are! April – Mum wants to speak to you. . ."

Two older girls were wandering our way, one reaching out a hand to take the mobile from Amber. I'd seen April and Ashleigh Bailey around before, but this close up, I suddenly realized how much they looked alike, from their blonde straightened hair to their perfect make-up; from their strappy short summer dresses to their flashy handbags.

"Hi Amber! Hi Rachel!" said Ashleigh, leaving April to chat on the phone. "How's your mum, Rach?"

As Ashleigh smiled a beaming smile in Rachel's direction, I realized something else . . . poor Amber really *did* look like the odd one out in her family. Even the *dogs* matched her perky parents and her sisters better than she did. Amber must have been feeling the comparison pretty badly too – she seemed to crumple her long legs and skinny arms into herself, as if she wanted to fold herself into invisibility.

"Yeah, my mum's fine," Rachel answered Ashleigh.

"Good!" Ashleigh beamed brightly some more, before turning her attention to her younger sister. "So, Amber; are you going to introduce me to your other friends? This wouldn't happen to be your date for the wedding, would it?"

TJ's eyebrows jerked upwards in surprise – Ashleigh meant *him*. From the grin on his face, it seemed like he was just about to come out with something funny, but didn't get the chance.

"God, *no*!" Amber blurted, flushing scarlet. "He's not. I mean, *they're* not. I mean, they're just some people from school . . . a couple of years below me. I . . . I don't really know them."

Oh.

OK, so Amber must've been a bit embarrassed about what her sister had just said, but did she have to be so, well, *rude*? Right in front of us? So much for feeling closer to Amber. And so much for Mrs S-T predicting that she would be a mate. (Only Mrs S-T had never exactly said that, had she? It was just me listening to her batty warblings and putting two and two together and getting forty-five. . .)

"Right, whatever!" Ashleigh shrugged, laughing lightly at Amber's awkwardness.

And right now, the awkward Amber rifled frantically in the bag by her side, pulled out a scruffy baseball cap and stuck it on her head, pulling the peak down low, low, *low* over her face.

"Hey, are you still in there, Amb?" Ashleigh laughed some more, trying to pull up the long funnelled peak. (Amber had yanked it so far down that practically only her chin was visible.)

"Mmm," Amber mumbled, from somewhere underneath her hat. "Just got that . . . that *thing* I get."

Me, TJ and Rachel frowned at each other, wondering what was going on with her.

"*What* thing?" asked Ashleigh, looking as confused as we were.

"That *thing*," we all heard Amber mumble from under her hat. "The photosensitivity thing. Need to hide from the light. . ."

I spotted Rachel scrunch up her nose in disbelief. Maybe it was time to go, since everything was getting seriously odd around—

"*NOOOOOOOOOOOOO!*" April's sudden yelp made us all jump. "Make her stop!! Mum! Mum – you'd better get here *quick*!"

You'd have thought Ellie was trying to set fire to Felix and Oscar from the hysteria in April's voice. It wasn't *that* bad.

OK, so heavy-duty patting with an ice-cream-covered hand had given Felix a messy Mohican, and thanks to Ellie sharing her cone with him, Oscar's entire muzzle was covered in sticky vanilla, but it wasn't anything that a quick wash and brush up wouldn't fix.

Only I could see a bit of a problem looming on the horizon.

Actually, the problem was a lot *closer* than the horizon. . .

"TJ . . . I think those people walking towards

us with the clipboards are judges," I whispered.

"The judges! Oh, April, Mum's going to have a fit!" gasped Ashleigh, flopping down on her knees and scooping up one of the mussed-up pooches.

Uh-oh.

"What? What have I done?" Ellie whimpered, staring imploringly up at us.

"Let's just go. . ." said TJ, holding both hands out to pull Ellie upright, along with what was left of her ice-cream cone.

As the four of us hurried off, I thought about glancing over my shoulder to see if there was a hint of a smile visible on Amber's face – same as there had been on Sunday. But I was too hurt by her brushing us off like that in front of her sisters, as if we were as pointless as nose hair.

"That stuff with Amber . . . I don't get it," grumbled Rachel.

"Me neither," said TJ.

"I know. Why'd she have to make out like we were nobodies?" I joined in, a pang of hurt squeezing in my chest.

"No, not *that*," said Rachel, shaking her head. "The photo-whatsit Amber was on about. That's where you can't stand sunlight – it brings you out in rashes and whatever."

"Yeah, so?"

TJ might have said it first, but it was exactly what I was thinking.

"*So* . . . why was she all right with the sun today, right until her sisters turned up? And I see her out and about in the sunshine all the time and she always seems all right. And another thing: if she's got photo-whatsit and that other stuff you said she told you about, Stella, how come I've never heard about it before, seeing as our mums are friends?"

I was taking in everything Rachel was saying, but it was the phrase "out in the sunshine" that wriggled another little thought into my head.

If agoraphobia was a fear of being outside or surrounded by strangers, how come Amber could leave her house and do stuff like serve in a busy café and come to crowded dog shows in parks?

It was all stranger than strange. . . .

Know your inner dog

I'm a poodle.

Well, I've got the curls for it, I guess.

I'm also easy-going, lively and affectionate. Oh, and apparently I love family life (yeah, except for when Dad's dismantled the toilet and forgotten how to put it back together and my brothers have eaten my favourite lipgloss).

I might not have got that What-type-of-dog-are-you? website address off Amber yesterday but after a trawl around the internet when I got home from the park, I soon stumbled across it, or at least something similar.

Once I'd found out that my inner dog was a poodle, I e-mailed the site to all my friends. It took most of the evening, but they all got back to me with their very own shaggy dog story. TJ turned out to be a Jack Russell (he wasn't too pleased with the size issue), Rachel was a Dobermann (beautiful but ferocious – spot on) and Megan was a Red Setter (the closest in doggy terms to Tigger). My old London buddies were a motley pack of feisty terriers (Frankie, Neisha, Eleni), a slim and sassy saluki (Parminder) and er, that was it (airhead Lauren said she couldn't work the test).

It was funny; Amber might have bugged me badly when she blanked us – and me in particular – in front of her sisters, but at least she'd ended up giving me a bit of entertainment last night. . . .

"'The Tiny Tea Cup'?!" scoffed TJ loudly, reading out the latest awful name idea on the specials board of the café. "That is *so* corny. Who'd come up with something as corny as *that*?"

"The old lady sitting at the next table," Amber said quietly, appearing by our table with her order pad. "Now what can I get you?"

Amber's head was tilted down, her eyes glued to the pad, her cheeks aflame. Was that redness down to her photosensitivity thing (probably not), or just 'cause she was embarrassed about blanking us yesterday (who knows), or just because she had to serve a lowly bunch of thirteen year olds (maybe)?

If I was a braver or more blunt person, I might have come right out and asked Amber why she'd turned so cold on us yesterday. But being a shy girl at heart, I opted to stay silent and uncomfortable.

"Doh," TJ mumbled, hitting himself on the side of the head with the nearest spoon now he realized he'd put his foot in it with the nearby old lady. "Should I just leave now?"

"No – she didn't hear you. She's too busy gossiping with her friend. So just order. The *waitress* is waiting."

Now Rachel; *there* was a braver, more blunt person. And she might have been talking to TJ but her eyes were boring into Amber, daring her to look at us. Or maybe she was trying to read Amber's mind and see what was going on with her and her strangely strange medical conditions.

"Um . . . can I have a Coke, please?" asked TJ.

"Same for me," snapped Rachel.

"Banana milkshake," I muttered quickly. "Um, *please*."

(Amber might have forgotten her manners yesterday but *I* was determined not to.)

Still blushing furiously and not making eye contact, Amber took a sideways step and started to take down "The Tiny Tea Cup" lady's order.

"Right – I'm going to go over there and put down some decent names," TJ said, in a low voice this time.

I watched for a few seconds as he walked over, grabbed the chalk and scribbled on the blackboard.

"*Rock 'n' Rolls*" (well, Phil sold seaside rock *and* sandwiches)

"*The Sea Anemone*" (Phil might like the name of the caravan Megan had stayed in)

"*The Sneezy Lemony*" (in case Phil fancied a truly daft name)

"*The Psycho Seagull*" (in case Phil fancied a truly psychotic name)

TJ seemed to be racking his brains for more inspiration while he was armed with his chalk. While he racked, my gaze drifted down to the pile of local history books I'd taken out of the library first thing this morning.

I couldn't do anything about the chandelier but this morning I'd got it in my head to try to find out more about what had happened to servant boy, Joseph, after he'd got his freedom from the Graingers.

"D'you suppose you'll find something about Joseph in there?" asked Rachel, starting to flick through the teen magazine she bought on the way here.

"Hope so," I mumbled, opening one book and starting to pore over ancient black and white photos.

Last week I'd seen a painting of Joseph as an adult, standing outside a shop with some kind of workman's apron on. Now I was determined to scour every old photo in these books, trying to spot his face, or read some kind of clue about the grown-up Joseph.

"He'd be easy to spot if he's in there, I guess. There weren't exactly too many black people around this area in the 1800s," said Rachel, leaning over for a look.

"Yeah, but photography just started happening after the 1860s, and only rich people could afford it, so who knows if he ever got his photo taken?" I mused. "Anyway, Mr Harper the librarian said I should try looking up Joseph's name in old newspaper files and stuff – he's got them all on computer. But the problem is, I don't know Joseph's last name."

"Where was he from, again? Barbados, wasn't it? So he'll have a last name from there."

"Yeah, but he or his family would originally have been brought over from Africa as slaves so his last name will be African."

It always gave me the wibbles when I spoke about black slaves and Barbados. I might never have known my grandad Eddie, but it was weird to think that a whole strand of my family went back to those hard-life, hard-to-imagine times.

"Um . . . that's not right, actually," a voice nervously chipped in.

It was Amber, hovering beside us, obviously listening in as she finished taking the order from the ladies at the next table.

"What's not right?" Rachel frowned up at her.

"Well, slaves might have had African names originally," said Amber, oblivious to Rachel's frown or maybe just pretending she hadn't noticed it. "But when they started working for the plantation owners, they were given *their* surnames instead. So Joseph was probably known as Joseph Grainger. I saw a programme all about it in . . . uh . . . erm . . . I'll just get everyone's order."

I think Rachel – acting as my beautiful-but-ferocious Dobermann guard dog – had frightened Amber off; not with a growl, but with a scowl.

It was a pity (for Amber) that she was frightened directly into the path of a bunch of customers bundling through the door. I swear she actually said "Eek!" as she found herself in Simon Riley's arms, a split-second after she'd bumped into him and nearly lost her balance.

"You OK?" laughed Si, letting her go.

All his indie/goth-y/grungey mates couldn't help laughing. (Except for the weird girl, Tilda, who didn't seem to be a big fan of laughing. Or even smiling. In fact, she seemed to be frowning – at Amber.)

And of course the more they laughed, the redder Amber glowed. In the few seconds it took her to get to the kitchen doorway and disappear she was as red as the rubble on Mars.

"Stop pestering the waitresses, Si!" Rachel called out cheekily to her brother.

"Get back to your comic, Rach, and mind your own business!" Si called back, just as cheekily.

The niggling between Rachel and Si carried on for another few niggles but I didn't hear any of them, as my mobile was beeping, alerting me to a call I'd missed.

"Stella? It's Jane Williams from the Portbay Journal – I interviewed you for the piece on Joseph's house."

How funny that the journalist felt she had to explain who she was. I mean, yeah, as if I was doing *so* many interviews with *so* many journalists that I needed reminding!

"I'm trying to track down your mother, and there's no answer at your home number. I need to speak to her as soon as possible about the message she left with my colleague – about the fantastic fund-raising idea she's had."

108

"What's up with you, Stella?" asked TJ, wandering back over to our table, wiping his chalky hands on his jeans.

"Seems like my mum's been keeping secrets," I mumbled, wondering where she was and what exactly she was playing at. . .

CHAPTER 11

Bright ideas x two

"Wow," muttered Mum, her dark eyes huge, taking it all in.

"I know," I said, with a grin a mile wide on my face.

There was no Jake and no Jamie around to spoil the moment with random biting and nose-jamming. There were no drills going off in the next room courtesy of Dad. In fact, right at this moment, Dad and the boys were back at home, busy bonding over a DIY box of Bob the Builder fairy cakes. Maybe we'd go home to a trashed kitchen, with two little boys on a sugar high terrorizing poor Peaches, but at least it meant me and Mum had uninterrupted us-time.

And unlike other mums and daughters, we weren't mooching around in some fancy shopping centre, checking out clothes or make-up or having a cappuccino or whatever.

There were no shops or cafés in Sugar Bay, just

a wide sweep of deserted beach, tumbling cliffs, and the old house. And so much for me never coming here again; Mum had helped me break her own rule, and come too – all because of the chandelier, and her brilliant idea to help save it.

"This place is *absolutely* stunning, Stella. I can't believe your dad and I have never visited it yet," said Mum, shading the warm, bright sun from her eyes and staring around the cove.

"Think it's a bit tricky with a double buggy," I laughed, nodding back up at the narrow, rambling stone path we'd scrabbled down to get here.

"Hmm. I guess we'll have to wait till the new development is built; they'll have to put a road in for that," muttered Mum, talking about the luxury holiday homes that were going to be plonked here soon. "Course, it won't look quite as amazing then."

"Nope," I said sadly, thinking of everyone I knew who loved this secret spot as much as me: TJ, Ellie, Mrs Sticky-Toffee, the psycho seagull, Peaches (I never guessed I'd be the owner of a sight-seeing cat). I suppose Amber had a soft spot for it too, since she'd run up to the headland and the view when she was miserable the other day. . .

"No wonder you've fallen for this house so

111

much," said Mum, focussing in on the old building, standing proudly (though crumbily) in the middle of its wildly overgrown garden. "It's just spectacular. Even past its best, it's *still* spectacular."

"I know. And now, thanks to you, we'll be able to save another bit of it before the bulldozers get here!"

"*Hopefully*, Stella," said Mum, shooting me a cautionary look. "You can have the best plan in the world and still not make something work."

"It'll work," I nodded at her, feeling as sure as the sky was blue and Peaches was weird that everyone would love her idea.

And this is what it was: the Sponsor a Crystal campaign, and the *Portbay Journal* were so up for it that they wanted run the story as soon as possible.

The whole thing had come to her this morning, Mum had explained, when she was clearing up shards of glass after Jake had broken her favourite vase by accidentally chucking a Teletubby at it. The plan was that everyone – from big businesses to little kids – could sponsor an individual crystal droplet on the chandelier, for however much they could afford. That way, the museum got their extra cash quick and then, once the chandelier was in place in the replica ballroom at the museum, a fancy board would go up with the names of everyone who'd been a sponsor.

Mum hadn't wanted to tell me about her excellent idea and get my hopes up until she'd run it by the girl at the newspaper and the director at the museum, and checked that *they* thought it was excellent too.

"So, will we go and try to get a look at the chandelier?" I asked her, dragging her attention away from the view to the reason we'd come here today.

"Yep, you lead on, since you know where you're going!"

And so I started heading for the house, with my feet slithering first in sand, then scrunching over shingle, then padding over the scruffy grass that led up to the rusty iron railings that must have once looked so imposing.

"Just got to wriggle through here," I mumbled, ducking through a gap where two railings had corroded clean away. "And watch out for the rose bushes – they're really pretty but they've got lethal spikes on them."

"Hey, Stella, remember when we used to read you the story of Sleeping Beauty? This is just like her enchanted garden. . ." I heard Mum say as she followed me through.

The garden of Joseph's house *was* kind of magical; full of towering purple foxgloves and tangling green ivy. Me and TJ, we'd set our Fake Fairy Project here, propping up the fairy paintings I'd done and photographing them. Rachel's mum had loads of them framed and up for sale in the Portbay Galleria. It was going to make us a fortune (yeah, *right*).

"OK, we're coming up to the main window of the ballroom," I explained, hoping Mum wasn't going to pay too much attention to the half-overgrown "*Dan . . . Keep Out*" sign we were passing. Unlike Ellie, I had a feeling that Mum might guess Dan's last name was "ger".

"Hmm . . . it does look pretty well boarded up to me, Stella," said Mum, resting her hands on her hips and surveying the handiwork of the men from the council.

"But Mum, maybe if we just get up to the window sill we'll be able to see through the cracks!"

I'm pretty sure that Louise Stansfield, the designer-dressed marketing executive, wouldn't have given it a go (too messy). And Mrs Stansfield, responsible mum of three, wouldn't have attempted it (too risky). But this afternoon, my mum acted like Lou, the teenager she once was, and leapt and clambered up to the ledge alongside me.

Breathlessly, we both leant our forearms hard down on the wide ledge and pushed the toes of our trainers into the wall, just to keep us up there.

"See anything?" Mum gasped, darting her head from board to board, searching for chinks that might let us peek into the ballroom.

"Nope," I panted, my feet scrabbling for a foothold. "Can't see a thing . . . . oh!"

And with that, I lost my grip and went slithering back down to the weed-covered ground.

"Ah, well," sighed Mum, letting go too and flopping gracefully by my side. "Pity we can't count the droplets properly. The newspaper will just have to estimate how many there are on the chandelier."

Zaaappppfff.

That was the sound of an idea blasting into my head. It wasn't just *Mum* who came up with them, y'know. . .

Twenty minutes later, my idea had taken us to the offices of the *Portbay Journal*.

". . .and *there* it is. Thanks, Nick!" said Jane the

reporter to the guy working the computer in front of us.

He'd just called up a photo of me, TJ, Rachel, Megan and Ellie in the ballroom of Joseph's house, the chandelier sharply in focus above our heads. It was the same picture they'd snapped last week and run in Saturday's paper.

"Oops – just a second, my editor wants me," said Jane suddenly. "But Nick can blow the image up some more, can't you, Nick?"

"No problem. Actually, let me zoom in so you can see *this* section better," offered the designer bloke, speedily clicking a few keys on his keyboard.

And by the magic of computers, he quickly enlarged just one part of the photo and let the new image fill the screen. Now we could have a much more detailed look at the chandelier.

"That's great!" said Mum, enthusiastically. "We're still going to be guesstimating how many droplets there are, but at least now it can be a bit more of an educated guess. . ."

Yep, taking a closer look at this recent photo had been my ace idea. But as I began counting the bottom layer of crystals, my eyes were drawn to a lone pane of glass in the window just behind it. The sun was streaming through the layered years of dust in the glass, but it looked like someone had made use of it. In the same way you get people writing "Wash me!" through grime on white vans, someone had carefully drawn out one word through the dust with their finger.

It said—

"Oh, come on, Jim! Please don't make me cover it!" I suddenly heard Jane pleading.

"It'll be a laugh, Jane!" the editor was booming breezily. "It's going to be the wedding of the year – no expense spared!"

"Yeah, you mean it's going to be the worst over-the-top, frilly, fancy do ever!"

"Maybe but some of the biggest families in town are going to be there, like the Baileys, so we *have* to cover it."

The Baileys? That made my ears prick up. They were talking about the wedding Amber was going to. Not that I cared any more about what Amber was up to. Not after—

Bleep!

At the café, said TJ's text. *Can u come? Amber's got something 2 show u. . .*

What is it? I texted back.

Come see 4 yourself! TJ zapped back infuriatingly.

I didn't know if I wanted to see anything Amber Bailey had to show me.

Uh-uh.

No way.

Then again, I didn't think my natural nosiness could keep me away from the café.

"Mum, do you fancy going for a coffee after this?" I asked her.

"Sure. . ." she mumbled, trying not to lose her concentration as she counted the crystals.

And then, once again, my eyes darted to the word drawn in the dust on the windowpane behind the chandelier.

It read *Willow*. . .

CHAPTER 12

Amber's big, fat, boy fib

I couldn't believe what I was looking at.

"1887; that's the date on the back," Amber was telling me.

The kitchen of the Shingles café might have been hot but I had shivers skittling up and down my spine.

It was just that face . . . *his* face. Joseph's dark eyes were staring out at me, his hint of a smile coming across more than a century.

"He looks about fifty, or maybe sixty there, don't you reckon?" said Amber, standing by my side and staring at the framed photo on the wall with me.

"Yeah . . . I'd've recognized him anywhere," I mumbled, hoping that didn't sound too dumb. It wasn't just that Joseph was the only black person in the gathering outside the church. It was the same secret smile and bright eyes I'd seen in the two paintings he'd been in; the Grainger family portrait as a boy, and as a young man in front of the old-fashioned shop he must've worked in.

I wished Mum could've come for that coffee and seen this with me. But on the way here from the newspaper office – right on cue – the call had come: Jamie had bitten Jake on the arm for eating the last Bob the Builder fairy cake and Jake had retaliated by tearing the head off Jamie's Noddy toy and dunking it in yoghurt. It was mayhem and Dad needed Mum to come quick. So I'd hurried to the Shingles café on my own and found myself being beckoned by Amber almost as soon as I arrived. "Wait till you see!" TJ had grinned at me, as I hesitantly followed Amber behind the counter and through to the kitchen area.

"Now be careful with that!" Phil bellowed in my ear, his hands bearing a stacked-high tray of dirty dishes. "That's a rare antique, that is! I paid a small fortune for that!"

"Um, OK," I nodded, whipping my fingers away so quickly from the photo it was as if the frame was electrified.

"He's only joking," Amber smiled at me once Phil had ambled off. "He bought that photo – and all the rest he's got up around the place – for a fiver!"

"A fiver each?" I asked, trying to add that up in

my mind. Apart from the ones hanging in the kitchen (gathering a thin layer of dusty grease, or greasy dust), there were plenty more displayed out front in the café and even a few in the loos.

"No, a fiver for the whole lot!" laughed Amber. "He bought a bundle of them at a car boot sale in Westbay years ago, when he took over the café. He thought they'd add a bit of local colour."

Staring at the photo, I felt freaked out round the edges. *Whatever Happened to Joseph?*: that was the headline in the newspaper last Saturday, right next to the feature about saving the chandelier. Jane the reporter had asked if anyone could help solve the mystery of where Joseph ended up, and now here I was, looking at another piece of the puzzle. A piece of the puzzle the owner and the waitresses of the Shingles café had walked by for years without realizing.

And it was freaky and amazing to realize that Joseph must have stayed in the area after all – so much for thinking that he could have travelled off anywhere in the world.

Another reason for feeling suddenly freaked out was that it dawned on me that my grandad Eddie would be nearly sixty by now, same as Joseph was in this photo. And what had happened to *him*? If I saw Grandad Eddie now, would I recognize him from the one snap I had of him at the fair, aged eighteen (with his arm around seventeen-year-old Nana Jones)?

Then Amber hit me with yet another wave of freakiness.

"Y'know, the bride's *got* to be Joseph's daughter. Her colouring's quite light but her eyes and her smile are the same."

"His *daughter*?" I gasped, straining my eyes at the young woman in the middle of the group of people. She was very pretty, with her hair tucked out of sight under a bonnet and wearing a dark long-sleeved dress that was nipped in at the waist, with wide skirts that brushed the stone steps she was standing on. But even though all these people were gathered outside a church, why did Amber think the woman was a bride, and that this was a wedding?

"Wearing white for a wedding was only for posh people back in those days," she said, reading my mind. "Ordinary people just wore their best clothes."

Amber really *was* the queen of interesting facts.

And as soon as she said that, I realized that of *course* it was a wedding party. The smiling couple in the middle, arm-in-arm; the proud relatives

122

posing all around them . . . you just needed to imagine them in modern-day clothes and it could be any wedding now.

But if that *was* Joseph's daughter, then Joseph's wife would be there too . . . how freaky was *that*? I needed to study this picture properly, which was tricky to do when you were in the way of every waitress scurrying by.

"I told Phil you'd be crazy about this photo," Amber chatted on. "So he said you could have it. It's not as if it's anything special to him, stuck through here."

Mum always brought me up to be polite, so I should've argued and said no, no, I couldn't possibly. But it really *wasn't* what I wanted to say.

"That's really nice of him," I murmured, lifting it gently from its hook. "And you. It was nice of you to . . . well . . . y'know."

A big dollop of shyness got me a bit tongue-tied there but from Amber's pink cheeks and chuffed smile, it seemed like she understood what I was trying to say.

Actually, there was something else I wanted to say.

"When do you get a break, Amber? Fancy hanging out?"

*

The inside of The Vault was like, er, a vault. A very *loud* vault that happened to have Dr Dre blasting out of vibrating black speakers.

I hoped all the gloom wouldn't stress Amber out, what with her suffering from SAD, and everything. . .

"I've never been in here before," said Amber, wide-eyed, as she stepped inside the dimness of Portbay's hip CD shop. "Never thought I was cool enough."

She jumped, then giggled as she nearly walked straight into a full-size cardboard figure of Legolas from *Lord of the Rings*.

"Hey, I wouldn't worry about being cool enough for this place. It's so dark in here that no one would notice if you were in the latest pair of anti-fit Levi's or a gorilla suit," TJ joked with her.

"Or maybe even a waitress's uniform," said Amber, wryly.

After she'd made such an effort with the photo of Joseph, TJ – like me – had put aside all thoughts of Amber's weird phobia stories and her blanking us at the dog show. Which is why he'd shrugged a quick "yeah, whatever" when I came out of the Shingles kitchen and announced to my friends that Amber would be tagging along with us during her break.

Rachel wasn't so keen to forget though, and stared at Amber warily as we headed over to the vintage comic section that TJ wanted to check out.

"Hey, brilliant: Buffy!" exclaimed Amber, reaching for a copy of the Vampire Slayer's magazine from a rack.

I was just wondering to myself what sort of free gifts you might get on the front of a magazine like that (a vial of fake blood? A miniature stake on a keyring?) when TJ asked a simple question and Amber came out with the strangest thing. . .

"Are you a big fan, then?"

"God, yeah. I *love* Buffy. Well, not so much Buffy as Willow."

Huh? What was with this Willow thing? It was like I was being haunted by a name. . .

"What's so great about W-Willow?" I said to Amber, trying to remember which character she was in the TV series, and struggling to stop the wibbles in my tummy translating into stammering.

"She's a computer student who happens to be a witch who has a girlfriend and then nearly destroys the world," TJ mumbled, giving me a quick synopsis while engrossed in the comic he'd just picked up. "Just your average girl, really."

"Yeah, well, I don't really care about the witch stuff," Amber shrugged. "I just like the fact that the actress who plays her is a red-head. I've got lots of pictures of her on this pinboard at home. I've even. . ."

I don't know what the end of that sentence was going to be: "I've even imagined myself playing that part in the TV programme"? "I've even thought about turning to magic and destroying the world too"? Whatever it was, the end of Amber's sentence disappeared into thin air as she glanced over at the counter at the far end of the shop and spotted Simon Riley. He was flicking through the pages of some magazine while a couple of his grungey mates looked on. I don't think he'd even noticed anyone was in the shop. We could probably stick a bundle of CDs and Legolas under our T-shirts and walk out of here and he'd still be flicking.

"Are you OK?" I asked Amber.

"Yeah . . . well, no," Amber replied, turning luminous pink in the dark. "I didn't see it was him there when I came in. I mean, I didn't know Rachel's brother worked here!"

"It's only for the summer. Or until the guy who runs the place gets fed up with all the sickies Si pulls and how late he wanders in," Rachel told

126

her. "God, you're not *another* one with a crush on him, are you?"

The blast of the hip-hop meant that no one outside of a twenty centimetre range would've been able to hear what Rachel just said. But Amber didn't seem to see it that way.

"No! I mean, *no!*"

And with a look of shocked embarrassment, Amber disappeared. It was as if a trap door had opened up and swallowed her into the cellar. Except she hadn't exactly been swallowed – she'd just crumpled herself down on to her haunches, still clutching her Buffy magazine.

"Er . . . it's OK. I don't think Si even noticed we're here!" I said, to the top of Amber's head.

Amber didn't look reassured, specially the way she'd hidden her head behind the magazine. I glanced at TJ and then Rachel, with "what do we do?" written on my face.

TJ gave a shrug, and crouched down on his knees beside Amber. I decided to follow. And with a loud, theatrical sigh, Rachel lowered herself down to our huddle too.

"Look," she said wearily, as we hunched between the magazine racks and the Thrash Metal H–Z section. "Are you *sure* you don't fancy my brother?"

"No, *honestly* I don't!" Amber insisted, coming out from behind the magazine to protest her innocence. "It's just that I *know* all his friends think I'm, like, *mad* on him or something. And it's *so* embarrassing!"

"But why would they think that?" I asked her.

"'Cause this morning when Si came into the café, I tripped right into him. And I've got his order wrong a couple of times. OK, well, *every* time," Amber admitted, her face practically strobe-ing pink. "Oh, and I tipped a bowl of sugar into his lap. I heard his mate Tilda say to the others that those were all sure signs that I fancied him."

"And you *definitely* don't?"

That was Rachel again, narrowing her eyes in Amber's direction.

"Absolutely not! I mean, your brother's kind of cute . . . in a sort of freaky way. But him and his friends have only really been hanging out at the café the last week or so. If they knew me better—"

"—they'd know you're that way with *everyone* you serve in the café?" suggested TJ.

"Mmm," nodded Amber, fidgeting on her haunches as she tried to get more comfortable or ward off cramp maybe.

Pity she knocked over a stacked display of *The*

128

Hitchhiker's Guide to the Galaxy with her elbow while she was at it. . .

As the books tumbled and clattered in slow motion, poor Amber looked just about mortified enough to *faint*. (At least she didn't have far to fall.)

Even above Dr Dre's loud droning, the thunderclap of tumbling books would've got Si's attention. And if Si (and his mates) clocked Amber hiding away and blushing so badly now, they'd probably have her down as a loved-up stalker for *sure*.

"Sorry – that was me!" I called out, jumping to my feet and gazing over in Si's direction. "I'll tidy them up!"

I don't know what suddenly made me take the blame for Amber's clumsiness; maybe it was pay-back for the framed photo I had tucked away in my bag just now.

"Yeah, and I'll help her!" said TJ, jumping up beside me.

Goodness knows what Si and his mates must have made of the two of us jumping up like Jack-in-the-boxes. But then again, from the bored look on his face, I don't think he really cared too much. His magazine and his conversation with his pals was *way* more interesting than us.

"Oh, thank you! *Thank* you!" Amber mouthed up at me and TJ, as she blushed the colour of red-sky-at-night and frantically started gathering up the fallen books.

As me and TJ got down on our knees to start re-stacking, I snuck a quick peek at Amber and had the funniest feeling that she was about five seconds away from crying.

OK, make that *one*.

"God, I am such a *klutz*!" she suddenly moaned, dropping her head on to her knees and letting sobs shake her shoulders.

"Hey, what's the deal?" Rachel asked, frowning in confusion at TJ, me and Amber. "So she knocked over a couple of books, so what? Or is she really *that* bothered what my stupid brother and his mates think of her?"

I was tempted to remind Rachel of just how crummy it felt to have everyone staring at you (and thanks to those *particularly* public fits she'd had, Rachel should know), but Amber was talking again.

Or at least, she was mumbling something soggily into her arms that we just couldn't *quite* make out.

"What? Tell your uncle TJ. . ." said TJ, leaning closer to Amber and sticking a kindly ear in her direction.

Cue more soggy mumbling.

"She said . . . uh, something about a juicer, I think?" TJ translated for us, with a puzzled shrug.

Wow, this conversation was getting more peculiar by the second. Chatting in a CD shop while crouching down was surreal enough, without juicers coming into it.

"I said a *loser*, not a juicer!" Amber corrected TJ, lifting her head up and giving us a glimpse of her tear-reddened eyes. "I am such a *loser*!"

"You're *not* a loser!" I said automatically, even though I didn't really know her well enough to be sure if that was true or not.

"Yes, I am!" Amber blurted out. "Even my own family think I'm a loser! They always try and act nice to me, but I know it's 'cause they feel sorry for me."

"Yes, but if they feel sorry for you, it's probably 'cause of all the conditions you have," I suggested.

"Yeah, I suppose. . ." Amber snuffled. "The thing is, I just end up telling them stupid, stupid stuff. . ."

"Like what?" Rachel frowned at her some more.

"Yeah, like what?" I asked, with my heart sinking. The vibrant shade of fuchsia that Amber was flushing, you knew the answer was going to be a doozy. . .

"Like . . . like I told them I was taking someone to my cousin's wedding on Saturday," she groaned.

"A *boy* someone?" asked Rachel, perking up at this twist in the conversation.

Ah, so *that* was why Amber's sister homed in on TJ as possible date material at the dog show. And I guess that's why Amber got all flustered and weird on us at the time. Cute as he was, at thirteen and shorter than average, TJ wasn't exactly ideal dating material for a fifteen-year-old, taller-than-average, easily embarrassed girl like Amber.

"Yeah, a *boy* someone," Amber admitted miserably. "Oh, but *your* mum's friends with *my* mum, Rachel – please, please, *please* don't say anything to her! If my mum knew I was lying. . ."

"But won't your mum know you were lying when Saturday comes and you've got no one to take to the wedding?" I asked, in as kindly a voice as I could (i.e. the opposite to the way Rachel would've sounded asking the same question). "I mean, you *don't* have anyone to take, do you?"

"No. My family keeps asking who it is, and I keep telling them that they'll have to wait and see. Anyway, that's why I've been trying to get out of going. But unless I get knocked over by a bus, or Portbay gets hit by an earthquake, I'm going to *have* to show up – with no boyfriend, and my mum and my dad and my sisters thinking I'm even *more* of a loser for lying about it. . ."

Uh-oh: the waterworks had started again. Drizzles of wet misery were coursing from Amber's auburn-lashed eyes, and one damp nostril.

"What *now?*" Rachel asked, sounding as softly sympathetic as a lump of granite in a freezer.

"I – I – want to leave here, but I don't know how to without Si and his mates seeing me. They're just *so* going to suss that it was *me* who knocked all the books over!"

"Oh, for goodness' sake," Rachel said irritably. "Right: Stella, you stay down here and tidy up the books; TJ, get ready to smuggle Amber out; Amber, keep down low till the end of the Hardcore Hip-Hop CD section, then run out of the door as fast as you can."

When she'd finished barking orders at us, we all just stared hard at her.

"And what are *you* going to do?" TJ asked her.

"Bug my brother stupid," Rachel answered matter-of-factly, getting to her feet. "To give you a bit of cover."

"Thank you. . ." Amber mumbled, pulling

herself together enough to let a small, grateful smile flicker Rachel's way.

"No problem. Any excuse to annoy my big-headed brother is fine by me," muttered Rachel, with a glint in her dark almond eyes as she straightened up. "So everybody, get going!"

TJ jumped to life, ambling across the floor towards the door, a casual(ish) whistle on his lips. Amber came scurrying behind, as low to the ground as her long gangly limbs would allow. And then as I tidied books furiously, I heard Rachel come out with a truly shocking statement.

Well, a statement that's truly shocking if you're a hyper-cool, pierced-lipped, black eyeliner-wearing, mega-gorgeous (in a slightly scary way), seventeen-year-old boy hanging out with his mates.

"Si? Si! I just remembered that Mum's got a message for you. . ."

"Oh, yeah?" Si called out to Rach. "What's that, then?"

"She says the tumble dryer is bust, so Eddie the Teddy won't be dry in time for you to take him to bed with you tonight. Hope that's OK."

Wow, that was below the belt. I didn't know if Eddie the Teddy even existed, or if Rachel had made him up, but the result was what she was after – i.e. toe-curling embarrassment.

As the laughter erupted and Si started roaring at Rach, I glanced sideways and saw the glint of a white apron bow disappear behind Legolas and out of the door into the sunlight. . .

CHAPTER 13

Megan's truly, madly *mad* idea

All the dumb, exciting, weird and wonderful stuff that can happen to you in a day .... it comes across as a whole lot less entertainingly dumb, exciting, weird and wonderful when you're telling it to people who have *no* idea what you're waffling on about.

Which is why I sat down at the computer this evening, all set to e-mail Frankie and the rest of my London buddies with my news and gossip, but ended up sending them each a cute e-postcard instead. And then I clicked straight on to Megan's address and waffled my news and gossip to *her*.

Of course, I filled Megan in with the big stuff first, like. . .

a) how she'd been right to suggest asking Mum for help with the Save The Chandelier campaign (straightaway, Megan offered to sponsor a crystal)

b) discovering the amazing framed photo of Joseph (which was currently propped up beside the computer, where I could stare at it while I waited for Megan's replies)

c) the latest Amber update (i.e. her big, fat, boy lie)

d) the story of Rachel winding Si up in front of his mates (*Can't BELIEVE she was so cheeky!* Megan had written. *Wait a minute; seeing as it's Rachel, yes I can. . .*).

With all that discussed, we were now in general waffling mode.

Hey, Megan: what goes 'squeet, poot, fnuuuuuuurrr'?

I have NO idea, Megan e-mailed me back. *Give me a clue. Is it something painful, or SCARY?*

Neither. It's Peaches, trying to get comfy on a balloon seagull, I keyed into the computer.

I leant over and peeked under the table at my fat cat, who'd finally settled down and stopped all that rubbery squeeting, pooting and fnuuuuurring. His upper body and head were snuggled into the balloon seagull that Mr Mystic Marzipan had twisted and squidged into shape for me. I just hoped Peaches didn't attempt that just-getting-comfy padding thing cats do with their claws – a loud bang that close up could wreck his feline eardrums for good.

Ahhhh, I should have guessed! Megan zapped

back. *Hey – here's one for you. Q: what SITS IN THE DARK, SNARLS and is DEMENTED?*

I don't know, but I don't think I'd want to run into one. . . I typed.

A: it's my sister Naomi. She's still in mourning for Rachel's brother and has now decided to become a recluse. She barricaded herself in her room today, with the lights out and the curtains shut, and has been playing very mopey music very LOUDLY!

OK, so I got the "sits in the dark" part of Megan's riddle. What about the rest? I read on. . .

Here's the DEMENTED bit: she's just playing this ONE track, over and over again. Think it's 'cause it's got this line in it that says 'I know I'll see your face again'. (As if! I mean, my parents are HARDLY going to rush back to Portbay on holiday with us after what happened!) And if Mum or Dad dares to ask her to turn the music down a bit, or tries to get her to come and have tea, she SNARLS at them to go away. Think she's trying to punish them for dragging her away from the love of her life.

I never thought I'd say this – considering the trouble she got us all into last week – but I couldn't help feeling sorry for Naomi. Si might have been a bit disgruntled when Megan and Naomi's family first left town but I'd seen him around a lot the last few days and he didn't exactly look like he was beside himself with woe.

Er, don't tell Naomi this, I wrote to Megan, *but Si doesn't seem to be moping much any more. He's back talking to Rachel (OK, QUARRELLING with Rachel), and he's been hanging out with his mates, in the café or in The Vault.*

Yikes – DEFINITELY won't tell Naomi that. She'd probably stay in bed for the next ten years. . .

"Hi, Stella – still on-line?" said Dad, suddenly appearing by my side in a slight haze of fine dust.

"Mmm, to Megan," I said, looking up at him and noticing that his bright blond hair was grey with plaster or concrete or whatever the fine dust was. "Do you need to use the computer?"

"Um, yeah . . . just need to look up some info on the internet about how to fix something I think I might have broken. . . But there's no rush."

He might have said there was no rush, but Dad had bodged so much of the DIY in this house so far that I didn't want to risk holding him up and having the boiler blow us all up in the middle of the night or whatever.

"I'll just say bye to Megan, and you can get right on," I told Dad.

"Great!" he smiled at me, nodding his head and sending more dust and a few gritty bits flying. "Give's a shout when you're done. . ."

As Dad padded off in his work boots – leaving a trail of muddy footprints that Mum was going to kill him over – I looked at the clock in the corner of the computer screen and got a surprise at how late it was, and how long I'd been e-chatting to Megan.

Megan, got to go . . . my dad needs—

But she beat me to it with another e-mail first.

Are you still there, Stella? What you told me about Amber –

(As I read Amber's name, Peaches began purring loudly in his sleep. You can call it a coincidence, but he'd done exactly the same thing whenever I'd keyed in Amber's name earlier.)

– about her having no one to take to the wedding . . . well, I've just had an ACE idea!

How intriguing, as detectives in historical programmes always say.

Yes, I'm still here. What's the ACE idea?

I waited, breath bated (whatever that is) for Megan's next e-mail.

Well, you said that Amber –

("Prrrrr!!" went Peaches)

– says she feels like a loser, right? So she doesn't JUST need to find a boy fast . . . she needs to find a COOL boy fast! That way, she'll feel GREAT in front of her family.

Uh, yeah, I tapped away, with a sinking feeling that this ace idea was going to be a bit pants. *But where's Amber –*

("Prrrr.")

– supposed to find a "cool" boy fast, Megan? This is Thursday, and the wedding's on Saturday. Do you know of an internet site that hires out cute but nice teenage boys? Or were you thinking she should just kidnap someone?!

KIDNAP!! What are you on about? I was thinking more of . . . BLACKMAIL!

Blackmail? Er, *who* was the demented sister in her family supposed to be again? Wow, you bet I couldn't *wait* to read what was coming next. . .

"Hey, Stella – sorry to rush you," Dad muttered apologetically but slightly urgently. "It's just that the thing I think I've broken is *definitely* broken and I better read up quick on a way to fix it straight away."

"Um, sure," I said, sliding out of the seat and trying to very quickly scan the rest of Megan's e-mail before I quit to let Dad in.

And the glimpse I had of it?

Well, what Megan suggested proved that she wasn't just ditzy – she really was truly, *madly* mad. . .

I spy a lie

Time: Friday morning. Place: the soon-to-be-renamed Shingles café.

Outside, tourists strolled along the prom in the sunshine, gulls swooped in the gentle summer currents, and Bob the dog snapped dopily at a passing bee.

Inside, Amber rushed around serving customers (the wrong things, I bet), me and TJ checked out the most recent suggestions on the specials board (we quite like "Phil's Phood", and quite hated "Taste-E-Grub"), and Ellie – who'd been offloaded by her mum on to TJ yet again – was counting each of the multi-coloured sprinkles on her cookie before she ate them.

"Thirty-five . . . *yum*. Thirty-six . . . *yum*. Thirty-nine . . . *yum*."

"It's thirty-*seven* – thirty-*seven* comes after thirty-six," Rachel's voice suddenly corrected her. None of us had spotted Rachel breezing in – though the jaws of a couple of teenage boy holidaymakers at the next table practically hit the deck as she pulled out a chair and sat down next to us. (Rachel didn't seem to notice – when you're probably the prettiest girl in town, being ogled at is no big wow, I don't suppose.)

"*So!*" said TJ, grinning knowingly at Rachel.

"So *what?*" Rachel answered, pretending she hadn't a clue what he was on about.

"*So*, what do you reckon – about Megan's idea?" I asked her, spelling it out in case aliens had erased her memory in the night and she'd forgotten all about it.

It had been pretty late yesterday evening, when I'd phoned and told my friends about the e-mail. TJ had burst out laughing and said, "No *way!*", while Rachel came out with, "Megan has *got* to be joking!!" before snorting so hard she had a coughing fit and had to go.

Megan's idea *was* kind of insane but last night, as I lay in bed, I kept thinking how brilliant it would be if it came off. Even when I met up with TJ this morning, he'd laughed about it in a different way, a "wouldn't it be funny if?" way.

And here was Rachel, looking super-cool in her posh sunglasses, her face giving nothing away. Did she still think it was the most nuts thing she'd ever heard, or did she think it might just work?

"Have you said anything to her yet?" she asked, nodding in the direction of Amber, who was taking an order from a table of grannies, unaware that a) she had a dollop of jam on her cheek, and b) Rachel might hold the key to her becoming a loser-free zone, for this Saturday at least.

"*Course* we've said something to her," said TJ. "'Two orange juices, a milk and a cookie, please!'"

"Ha *ha*!" said Rachel, without raising her mouth into anything that might hint at a smile, let alone a laugh. "You *know* what I mean."

"No – no, we haven't said anything about *that*," I reassured her.

"Good."

Er, I didn't much like the way Rachel was staring daggers at Amber. What was up with her? She'd seemed happy enough to help Amber escape from The Vault yesterday. So what was with the stony face now?

"What's going on, Rachel?"

"What's going *on* is that Amber Bailey is a liar and I don't really see why we should help her."

"A *liar*!" I whispered in disbelief. "What are you on about, Rach?"

"I spoke to my mum about some of the stuff she's been saying."

"What?!" I gasped, feeling my cheeks suddenly

144

blush in sympathy with Amber. "About the whole wedding and the boy thing?! But she asked you not to tell!"

"No – not *that*," said Rachel, shrugging her shoulders. "I spoke to my mum about all those illnesses and stuff that Amber's supposed to have. It's been bugging me, so I asked if Mrs Bailey had ever said anything about them to *her*."

"And what did your mum say?" asked TJ, keeping one eye on Amber moving about the café in case she got too close for gossiping comfort.

"Mrs Bailey says the family knows none of it's really true – they think Amber just comes out with it for attention. They kind of humour her and don't take it seriously."

Urgh. Well, that kind of made sense, since Amber's strangely strange "conditions" didn't.

"Anyway, that makes her a liar, doesn't it?" said Rachel, folding her arms across her chest. "*And* a bit of a saddo. . ."

"What's a 'saddo'?" asked Ellie, crinkling up her nose at us.

"Shush, Ellie," said her big brother. "Yeah, Rach, but maybe Amber *does* have all that stuff wrong with her, and her family are the bad guys, 'cause they don't believe her!"

"Oh, yeah? Well, let's see . . . she's supposed to

be 'photosensitive', but like I said before, I don't see her covering up or breaking out in a rash every time she's out in the sun," said Rachel, her dark eyebrows arched above her sunglasses as she spoke. "And that SAD syndrome thing; let's face it, Amber's miserable whether it's winter *or* summer. Agoraphobia – she definitely doesn't have *that* or she'd be stuck indoors hiding away from everyone all the time. And the dyslexia thing is probably one big lie too!"

I wasn't exactly sure how I felt about what Rachel had just said. Maybe I thought it sounded sort of crazy, or kind of pathetic, but I wasn't as tight-lipped *angry* at Amber as Rachel seemed to be. What was with her? I guess it was just her old intolerance shining through; the intolerance that made me wary of being friends with her at first. It was a side to Rachel that got on my nerves, to be honest.

"I mean, how would Amber like it if she had a *real* illness! One that she might have for the rest of her life?"

Oh, OK . . . suddenly I got it. Rachel was still living under the cloud of discovering she had epilepsy – the fact that someone was making up or faking an illness would be enough to make her good and mad, I guess.

146

"TJ. . ." Ellie piped up, in the midst of our grown-up conversation.

"Shh a second," TJ urged her, probably thinking she was after another cookie or something. "We're talking about big stuff just now."

"But TJ. . ."

"Look, if you need the toilet, Ellie, just go!"

"It's not that, TJ!" Ellie whispered, her eyes bright with a secret. "*Amber's* coming over!"

Bless her; Ellie wasn't worried about cookies and loo visits – she was worried about Amber catching us talking about her.

"Hi!" Amber smiled shyly, pulling up a spare chair from a neighbouring table. "Got a break for ten minutes."

"Uh, great," TJ mumbled, with a half-hearted smile on his face.

Amber glanced around at us all, and seemed to sense something was up.

"Listen, I'm really sorry I got all . . . y'know . . . *upset* on you guys yesterday," she said, her cheeks pinking up nicely. "Everything's been getting on top of me recently. But thanks for letting me hang out with you, and for helping me get out of The Vault."

She beamed her thank-you smile in particular at Rachel, who gave a quick *whatever* shrug in reply.

"Are you feeling better today?" I asked Amber, hoping I sounded vaguely normal.

"Well, I feel totally sick about the wedding tomorrow, and there's nothing I can do about my family thinking I'm a total idiot."

I didn't dare glance over at TJ. If we'd been able to pull Megan's idea off, Amber wouldn't be looking like an idiot at all. But without Rachel's help, it was never going to happen. . .

"Anyway, I've decided that at least I'm not going to *look* like a total idiot. Mum's still trying to talk me into this dress she wants to buy for me from the boutique in the High Street, but I'm just going to wear my best black trousers and a stripy top I got in the sales last year."

As she was speaking, Amber began pulling a whole bundle of neatly cut bits of paper out of her apron pocket.

"That's good," I said, talking about her wedding outfit but keeping my eyes on the bits of paper, each with one word neatly handwritten on them.

"What's this?" asked Ellie, pointing a sticky finger over random words like "Tasty", "Juice" and "Nibble".

"Oh, it's just a stupid idea I had," said Amber shyly, "to maybe help me come up with a new name for the café."

148

"How does it work?" Curiosity getting the better of him, TJ dropped the fake smile and leant over the muddled swirl of words for a better look.

"Well, I got the idea from something our art teacher told us about – this weird style of art in the 1920s or something, called the Dada movement."

"Dada?" giggled Ellie.

"Sounds silly, doesn't it?" Amber smiled at her. "But the people who were into it wanted a silly name. And they did silly stuff like writing down heaps of words on bits of paper, muddling them up, and then whatever they ended up with was this mad kind of poem!"

Amber was already fiddling with her bits of paper, putting three words together at a time.

"So I decided to scribble down lots of types of food, and words to do with eating, and see what happened."

"Can I try?" asked TJ.

"And me?" piped up Ellie.

"Of course!" smiled Amber. "We can *all* do it!"

I couldn't resist, and reached to pull out a few scraps of paper to play with. Rachel sat silent and kept her arms firmly folded over her chest.

"What've you guys come up with?" asked TJ. "I've got 'Big Spoon Munch'. I quite like that!"

"I've got 'Sweet Melon Burger' – yuck!" giggled Ellie.

"Mine is . . . 'Hot Pepper Jelly'," said Amber. "What's yours, Stella?"

Mine was nowhere near as cute or silly as theirs and had three words so long that Phil would need to extend his sign over the neighbouring shops if he wanted to use it (which he definitely wouldn't). I was just about to read it out when something pinged in my head so loudly that I couldn't believe the others wouldn't hear it. It's just that "Scrumptious Lasagne Delicious" – weren't they the sort of words you might struggle with if you were dyslexic? You'd maybe find it hard to spell them properly and write them as neatly as they were here. . . Poor Amber – she might be smart about lots of stuff, but she wasn't very good at making her own fibs believable.

Keeping my head bowed over the table, I flicked a sideways glance towards Rachel. I could just make out her eyes behind the dark brown lenses – she was staring back at me and thinking exactly the same thing.

"'Hot Pepper Jelly'?" Phil suddenly boomed above us, reading Amber's Dada name. "*Hot . . . Pepper . . . Jelly. . .* That's pretty good! No one's going to forget *that* in a hurry. I quite like

'Rock 'n' Rolls' too, though. Hey – *I* know! EVERYONE – LISTEN *UP*!!!"

The babble of chit-chat and tinkling of plates stopped dead, as the customers and waiting staff turned to see what Phil had to say.

"Got the new name of the café narrowed down to two choices I want to run by you all," he boomed. "Cheer and clap for the one you like the best. And let's start with 'Rock 'n' Rolls'!"

"That's *yours*!" I said to TJ, as if he needed any reminding.

There was a good smattering of claps and cheers (the cheers were mostly from our table), and some puzzled shakes of the head from various grannies who didn't get the puns.

"Great! OK, and how about 'Hot Pepper Jelly'!"

More clapping and cheering (from us again – well, fib queen or not, it was hard to be mad at Amber when she looked so absolutely and completely and pinkly chuffed).

"Well, I reckon Hot Pepper Jelly *just* pipped it there, folks!" Phil announced, grabbing Amber's limp arm and holding it aloft like she'd won a prize fight. "C'mon, Amber – get over there and rub the other names off the board, 'cause *yours* is the WINNER!"

There was a babble of comments and a ripple of applause around the café as everyone heard Phil's loud proclamation (the grannies still looked perplexed).

There was also a very good question, called out from TJ.

"So, Phil – what does Amber win, then?"

"A three-course meal on the house!" Phil announced, throwing his arms wide.

Everyone groaned and laughed – it would be a great prize for most people, but for a waitress who ate at the café for free all the time, it was about as exciting as an airline pilot winning a flying lesson.

Not that Amber seemed to mind – she sat glowing vividly pink, her face a mixture of embarrassment and pride.

"I've never won anything before!" she said, turning to us with a hint of pleased tears in her eyes.

"Amber? Can I speak to you for a second?"

I turned to see who was asking the question . . . and would have fallen off my chair if my bum hadn't been firmly plonked dead centre.

Si Riley was poking his head around the café door, a bag on his back (must've been en route to his job at The Vault) and a confused look on his face (guess he was wondering what the commotion in the café was all about).

Amber's expression read PANIC! She was frozen to the spot, fiery-cheeked. Thankfully, a gentle tap on the shin from my trainer broke the fear trance she was in, and in a flurry she babbled, "Uh . . . yeah. . ." and followed Si as he beckoned her outside.

"What's going on?" I muttered, watching as Si smiled and chattered, Amber stood and stared wide-eyed, and Bob shuffled over to them both and gazed up in the hope of a pat.

"What do you *think's* going on?" said Rachel, breaking her long silence at last. "He's offering to be her date for the wedding tomorrow."

"But from the way you were talking about Amber five minutes ago, I didn't think you'd done it!"

"Stella, I never *said* I didn't do it. I asked Si about it after you called last night. He said yeah. Course, that was before I knew Amber was such a liar, but that's *Si's* problem. . ."

"He said yes, just like that?" I asked in disbelief. "I mean, he was OK about you *blackmailing* him?"

Yep, Megan's truly, madly mad plan had been to get Si Riley to take Amber to the wedding – by blackmailing him over the tricky little cider secret. Rachel's parents had no idea that he a) had been spotted by all of us drinking underage, and b) had got Megan's sister Naomi glugging back the stuff and making a fool of herself too.

"Didn't need to blackmail him. Didn't get that far," said Rachel, drumming the fingers of one hand on her arm as she watched her brother through the window. "I just told him how Amber had lied about taking a boy to the wedding and how her family were going to tease her stupid if she ended up being on her own, and blah, blah, blah, and he said fine, he'd do it."

"But why was he so up for it?" I asked, my head riddled with confusion. "It's not like he knows Amber that well. And I thought he'd be too cool to do something like that. Without getting his arm twisted, I mean."

"Listen, my brother is a *boy*, and since he's a boy, of *course* he's annoying and an idiot."

"Gee, thanks!" laughed TJ.

"But he's OK underneath. Plus, if you hadn't noticed already, he likes to shock."

"What, the pierced lip, black eyeliner and T-shirts with skulls and swearwords are meant to *shock*?!" TJ joked.

"Yeah, and he really loves the idea of turning up to the straightest, fanciest wedding with Amber, just to freak out all the toffee-nosed town bores that'll be there," Rachel snorted. "It just depends if Amber's up for that. . ."

From the big smile that was spreading across Amber Bailey's face right now, it was pretty clear she was most *definitely* up for shocking the wedding guests too. . .

ChapteR 15

"Ja, ich bin aus, er, Norfolk. . ."

Y'know, it's hard to remember a time when our family didn't smell of nappies and dribbles of milk, but it did exist.

Those were the days when Mum bought expensive perfume for herself, and our house too. Those were the days when my parents got a babysitter in to look after me and would go out for expensive meals in posh restaurants, or to see trendy bands in cool clubs. If you haven't already guessed, those were the days before the twins arrived.

"It's fantastic, isn't it?" said our neighbour Margaret, holding up the front page of the local paper with the Sponsor a Crystal campaign plastered all over it.

It *was* fantastic. It was so fantastic that Dad had decided to take Mum out for a meal to celebrate, and asked Margaret to babysit (I refused to do it again after that first night in Portbay, when my brothers woke up and wrecked my room more than it was already wrecked).

But going out on the town post-twins – and in Portbay – wasn't as glam for Mum and Dad as in the old London days. For a start, getting dressed up involved Dad putting on a clean T-shirt and washing the plaster dust out of his hair, while Mum clipped sparkly hair clips in *her* hair (borrowed from me) and ironed a top for the first time since we'd moved here. And then off they'd gone, for a non-wild night out at the newly named Hot Pepper Jelly.

So far, I'd had a non-wild but quite nice night watching telly, chatting to Margaret, and showing her the photo of Joseph and the wedding party. Margaret was really interested; a few weeks back, she'd given me an old newspaper she'd found in her loft. It was dated 1930, and had this amazing photo of Elize Grainger in it, sitting in our garden, painting watercolour fairies, drinking tea and celebrating her hundredth birthday. The article was now pinned up on my board in the den – where Joseph's photo would be going too, out of grabbing (and doodling-on) range of Jake and Jamie.

"It's strange to look at people in old photos, isn't it?" Margaret mused, gazing at the wedding party some more. "Some faces look so of-their-time . . . and some seem so very familiar, as if you could pass them by in the street tomorrow."

Margaret might have sounded a bit teacher-ish and formal when she said that (well, she *was* a retired teacher so I guess she was entitled to), but I totally got what she was saying. Joseph's wife, for example, looked like any white-haired old lady you might see strolling along the prom – if you swapped the big Victorian frock for beige slacks and a nice cardie, of course.

"And you find yourself looking at these faces, wondering what they were like," Margaret chatted on, still lost in the photo. "Was this person a good musician? Was that person a funny storyteller? Was this person a terrible liar? You could spend ages trying to imagine their lives!"

I might have hung around and nattered away with Margaret for hours, the two of us making up secret life-stories for every face in the photo. But something she'd just said was burrowing into my head: "Was this person a terrible liar?" It got me thinking about Amber all over again. I'd wanted to like her . . . I *did* like her (she was kind of quirky and interesting) . . . but I couldn't get over the fact that she'd lied about her "illnesses" and lied (to her family at least) about having a boyfriend to take to the wedding. Did she lie about *everything*? Like all that stuff she seemed to know so much about; for instance, did women however-long-ago *really* use poisonous lead in their make-up, or was that just another story too?

"Scuse me, I forgot I promised to call my aunt in London tonight," I said to Margaret, as I pushed myself off the sofa and headed towards the hall.

I hadn't promised to call Auntie V at all, but she was the exact person I wanted to talk to right now.

"So, yes, Stella my little star, women really *did* use lead in their make-up, and yes, it really *did* rot their faces. Nicely gruesome historical fact, that, isn't it?" said Auntie V, in her usual, breezy, breath-of-fresh-air way.

I'd just spent the last few minutes telling her all about Amber and the confusion ping-ponging around my head.

"And listen, darling, I wouldn't judge this Amber girl too harshly. It sounds as if she feels very un-special indeed, and has invented all these illnesses or whatever just to give herself, well, a bit more of a 'hook', you might say."

"A 'hook'?"

"You know, an added something to her personality, to make herself more interesting."

"But she's pretty interesting as it is . . . she knows so much stuff about, well, *stuff*," I mumbled, thinking of the fun what-dog-are-you quiz we'd all done.

"Well, she's obviously not aware of that, and no one's tried to let her know," suggested Auntie V.

"But . . . but it's still *lying*, right?" I asked her, as I knelt by my bedroom window, watching single seagulls soaring and flocks of starlings whirling in the peachy-mauve evening sky.

"In this girl's case, let's call it 'inventing', not lying. I mean, we've *all* done things to make ourselves feel more interesting, especially when we're growing up. What about the time your dad told the kids at his school that his hair had turned white because he'd seen a ghost?"

"He *did* that?" I giggled.

Thump!

(That was Peaches, leaping up on to my bedroom window sill from the kitchen roof. He had some kind of long leaf in his mouth.)

"Oh, yes!" laughed Auntie V. "For one thing, I suppose it's more interesting than explaining his hair was bright blond because of genes, and for another, he was getting teased by some of his classmates about it and suddenly the ghost story made him sound so *very* cool. The flaw in his story, of course, was that *I* would've had to have seen the same ghost too!"

(Peaches was rubbing his face against my hand. I tried stroking his head, but it didn't seem to be what he was after.)

"Did you get teased about being different too?" I asked Auntie V, thinking how I'd worried about looking different in my own way when I arrived in Portbay. Afro hair – even my golden-brown version – was a bit of a novelty here.

(It dawned on me what Peaches was after: weird cat that he was, he wanted me to play with the leaf the way a dog likes you to pull at the stick he's got locked in his jaws.)

"Absolutely – but I loved being different! I still had a go at inventing too, though. I remember sitting on the bus once with my friend when I was about your age, talking terrible German, calling each other German names, and hoping everyone would think we were hopelessly attractive foreigners. Of course it didn't work, since we lived in rural Norfolk and every single passenger on the bus knew we were Vanessa and Janey and not 'Gertrude' and 'Ute'."

Hmm. I guess now that she'd said that, I vaguely remembered something that me and Frankie did when we were nine – it had seemed like a good idea at the time, but I don't think our teacher was in the least bit convinced when we said we were late because we'd helped capture a runaway lemur from London Zoo. We just thought it would be much more exciting to say that, instead of admitting that we'd been playing a game of trying to push each other in puddles and had forgotten the time.

Maybe Auntie V was right; maybe I shouldn't think too badly of Amber. . .

(Suddenly, after happily playing "tug" with the leaf, Peaches yawned and let it go.)

"Stella? Stella? Are you still there? You've gone very quiet!"

Yes, I was still here, staring down at the long leaf I was holding between my fingers.

And the reson I was quiet was because I was thinking; thinking that tomorrow, I'd have to check out a tree book in the library, 'cause I had a funny feeling the leaf that Peaches had given me was from a willow. . .

162

The Great Make-*under*

Arboriculturist: that's . . .

  a) the name of a tree expert

  b) probably very hard to spell if you're a true dyslexic (unlike Amber)

  c) a word that would've taken me twelve years to try and say, back when my stammer was at its worst.

By the way, point c) is only funny 'cause I'm a stammerer (even if I'm more of a recovering stammerer) and I'm allowed to make jokes about it, even though no one else is. It's like TJ; only *he* can come out with something like "Look out; it's the pavement! Someone pass me a stepladder. . ." – I wouldn't *dare*. . .

Anyway, back to arboriculturists. Mr Harper the librarian had pointed me in the direction of a book by one, before whistling a jaunty tune and tap-dancing off to stack shelves. You know, I thought libraries were supposed to be quiet? It

163

was kind of hard to concentrate on the leaf drawings with all that pitter-patter, clippetty-clattering going on.

Mind you, *I* could speak. I was just muttering a *"yesssss!"* to myself as I matched the leaf in my hand to the picture of the willow on page 192, when my phone jingled loudly into life. Luckily, everyone in Portbay seemed to have better things to do than hang about in a library at half-nine on a Saturday morning, so I had the place to myself. (Though there was a faint whiff of something sweet in the air – had I just missed Mrs Sticky Toffee, mulling over books called *How to be Eccentric*, or *Fairy cakes for Seagulls* maybe?)

"Hello?" I said softly, gazing over at Mr Harper in case he was planning to tell me off for talking on the mobile, whether the place was empty or not. Hurray – I could hear him (tip-tip-tapping) somewhere at the far end of the room, so I knew I should be safe for a second or two.

"It's me," said Rachel. "Something bad's happened. I mean, *BAD* bad."

"W-what?" I blurted, feeling adrenalin whoosh around my body in a panic. Had Rachel just had another epileptic fit? (Duh . . . she'd hardly be on the phone if *that* was the problem.)

"I'm at my mum's shop. Amber's just walked

164

in – and she needs help. You've got to meet us at my house as soon as you can. And call TJ to come too, 'cause this is a state of emergency."

"But . . . but what's the emergency? And how come you're helping Amber? I thought you couldn't stand her?"

Rachel sighed a short, sharp sigh that I instantly decoded.

"Amber's standing right beside you, so you can't talk, right?"

"Right. And Mum's just offered to drive us to my house so I've got to go."

"OK – I'm coming. . ." I mumbled, hurrying to close my book and stuff it back on the correct shelf. As I hurried, the framed photo in my bag thudded against my hip. It was Joseph's photo, and however much I loved it, I'd decided something after showing it to Margaret the babysitter last night – I needed to let other people see it too. Which is why I'd been on my way to the museum with it, to see if they wanted to think about using it in a display about Joseph and Elize, alongside the locket.

In fact, last night, I'd got thinking that *all* the things I'd collected to do with Joseph and Elize: the cutting from the 1930s newspaper; the original flower-fairy watercolour; the box with

Elize's initials handcarved on it; the brass button inside that I was sure belonged on the uniform Joseph wore as a child servant . . . all of it might end up being handed over to the museum.

But those historical decisions could wait. Right now I needed to get to Rachel's and find out what modern-day disaster had happened to Amber. . .

"Nunghhh. . ."

It was a kind of grunt of surprise and moan of pain at the same time. But it was all that TJ seemed to be capable of, when he arrived at Rachel's house about two seconds after I did and saw the state Amber was in. Even Bob was alarmed; his tail was firmly tucked between his legs.

I'd already got over my initial surge of shock and horror – now I was just feeling a huge wave of pity for Amber.

"I know, I know," Rachel nodded at TJ. "My mum is best friends with Mrs Bailey, and even *she* can't believe what a mother could do to her own daughter!"

Wow, what a turnaround from yesterday, when Rachel had had such a downer on Amber. I guess the mess Amber was in had finally squeezed a little sympathy from Rachel's rock-like heart.

Then again, I guess Amber's predicament was something style queen Rachel couldn't resist: sorting out a fashion disaster.

As Rachel talked, Amber sat silently on the sofa, too traumatized to utter a word. And no wonder: she'd been the victim of the worst makeover I'd ever seen. (Trust me, I'd seen a few; Frankie and me used to *love* slagging off terrible makeovers in her mum's magazines.)

"Here . . . here, Amber!" I said, rifling in my pocket and finding a Kit-Kat I'd bought on the way to the library and forgotten to eat. "Mrs Sticky Toffee once told me that sugar is good for shock!"

My words had an effect, even if the Kit-Kat didn't. Amber shook her head, sending huge waves of hairsprayed hair bobbing.

"You're not meant to give people in shock anything to eat or drink – you're just meant to get them to lie down," she said, dropping one of her interesting facts into the conversation on autopilot, even though she looked just about ready to curl up and die.

"I think *I* need to lie down," TJ said, frowning at the vision in front of him. "What *happened* to you, Amber?"

"Her mum insisted she came into the salon, so

167

she could get 'ready' for the wedding later," Rachel jumped in and explained. "But basically, it was an excuse to get her hands on Amber and give her a makeover."

"Look, I don't really know a lot about this stuff," said TJ, "but aren't makeovers meant to make you look *better*?"

"And not like a man in drag?" Rachel said cruelly, but, er, accurately.

I'd seen drag queens on TV; two-metre tall blokes in jokey big wigs, plastered-on make-up and sequinned dresses, stomping around a stage in high heels, having a ball impersonating women. It was a pity that Mrs Bailey had turned her fifteen-year-old daughter into one (and a pretty lousy ad for her hair and beauty salon too. . .).

"She said I'd feel a lot more glamorous," Amber mumbled. "But I feel like a *right* kipper. . ."

And that's when TJ lost it; bursting out laughing at Amber's predicament.

And I mean, no wonder. Mrs Bailey had untied Amber's ratty red pigtails and puffed her hair up into a curly, hairsprayed bouffant. The make-up – pink, shimmery lipstick and matching pink eyeshadow – made Amber look like an albino bunny. Her bitten nails had been transformed into long pink claws, thanks to the wonders of false

168

nails and glue. And she hadn't got away with wearing her black trousers and simple stripy top – oh no. Amber had been forced into a hideous, shimmery, shapeless, lime-green dress with a ruffle at the neck.

Omigod.

What with her hair and her dress . . . she looked like a carrot. An albino carrot. An albino carrot in drag.

It was all getting too hysterical (in a bad way), which is why I found myself giggling (hysterically) alongside with TJ.

"Look, it's *not* funny!" said Rachel. "Amber came to my mum's shop for help, 'cause it was closest to the salon. She had to escape while her mum was off looking for a padded bra for her!"

Rachel was trying to be supportive. But as she said the last part of her sentence, even *she* couldn't help hearing how ridiculous her words were and starting snorting and sniggering too.

For a second, Amber looked like she might cry . . . but then a grin started playing at her sugary-pink lips and she began pinging her nails back one-by-one, hurtling each fake talon in the direction of the bin.

"Who cares!" yelped Amber. "I'm not going to this stupid wedding anyway!"

"Oh, yes you *are*!" barked Rachel, dropping the giggles and getting serious again. "You're going to go; you're going to go with my brother, and you're going to look *great*!"

"But how?" asked the albino carrot.

"'Cause you're about to get a make-*under*," muttered Rachel, narrowing her eyes and looking like she meant business. . .

CHAPTER 17

What-a-phobia?

Amber's mobile mewed again.

"I'm switching it off," she mumbled, pressing the off key. "I've told my mum I'll be at the wedding later, so I wish she'd leave me alone!"

Speaking of parents, my dad is always pretty on-the-ball when it comes to music and trends and stuff. He likes books with covers that look very hip but obscure. He raves about modern Iraqi movie-makers, and arty documentaries on BBC4 (not that you can see many modern Iraqi movies or *get* BBC4 in sleepy Portbay).

But what my dad really, *really* likes (and this'll embarrass him horribly), are all those *I ♥ the '70s* type shows you get on TV. He grew up in the 1970s, and he regularly bores me stupid with stories about how ace things like Chopper bikes and Wagon Wheel biscuits were. (Huh?)

But as we sat watching Rachel transform Amber from an albino bunny to a sort-of swan, a

Saturday morning TV show my dad had wittered on about pinged into my brain. It was called *Swap Shop*, and it was where kids phoned in with stuff they wanted to get rid of, in exchange for stuff they *did* want. And thanks to a raid on Rachel and her mum's wardrobes, Amber had swapped practically everything she'd arrived here in for something a hundred, probably a *trillion* times better. . .

"We still need jewellery," Rachel announced, sliding another washed and hairspray-freed rope of red hair between straighteners.

"I've got a little bracelet in my bag. . . Mum didn't let me wear it," Amber said, inclining her head towards Rach.

"Hold still," Rachel ordered her. "Fine – if your mum didn't like it it'll probably be great. But we still need a really cool necklace. TJ – can you grab the jewellery box on my mum's dressing table?"

"Can't Stella get it?" he wimped out.

"*Stella*," I said, "is doing Amber's nails, if you hadn't noticed!"

They might be bitten and short, but Amber's nails were getting a file and a swoop of clear varnish on them anyway.

"Yeah, go get it yourself, TJ!" Rachel said fearsomely. "Quick, quick!"

"But what does a jewellery box look like?"

"Like a box. With jewellery in it," Rachel sighed. "Look, stop being such a wimp, TJ – I'm not asking you to rummage in my mum's underwear drawer or anything!"

I know TJ wanted to help, but he was finding the girliness of the make-under pretty hard to handle, I think – specially since him and Bob kept getting ordered out of the room when Rachel was trying different outfits on Amber.

"What's he *like*?" muttered Rachel distractedly, as she straightened away.

"Nice," said Amber, smiling gratefully.

"Yeah, he's all right," Rachel agreed, pretending to sound reluctant. "Even if he's so thick that he doesn't understand what a stupid box looks like. . ."

"Hey, I heard that!" TJ appeared in the doorway of Rachel's room, clutching a square wooden box with silver inlays indented into it. "Is that any way to speak to a friend?"

"Well, a useless friend like you, maybe!" Rachel grinned.

Like I said before, I'm not brave, and I'm not blunt. Usually. But as TJ and Rachel bantered, I suddenly figured that if *Amber* was going to be our friend too (and it looked like she was), we'd have to get a few things straightened out first.

173

Time to take the plunge (and do it straight away, before I bottled it. . .).

"Amber?" I began, glancing up from her nails. "How come you made up all those illnesses you're supposed to have?"

The room went ominously quiet, except for Bob's happy panting. Rachel's hand was frozen in mid-air with the straightening irons. TJ was (unusually) silent, except for one loud gulp. For a second, Amber looked like I'd slapped her in the face, and left a scarlet flush of a mark there on her cheek.

"I – I – just did it. Made stuff up, I mean. Every time one of my sisters went on about *another* great exam result, or spoke about *another* compliment they'd been given, or introduced *another* great boyfriend to my mum and dad . . . I just went on the internet and found some condition thing I thought I could have."

"Just to get sympathy?" asked TJ.

"I guess." Amber shrugged, looking like she wanted the ground to open up and swallow her blushing self. "It was a dumb idea . . . and *then* I didn't know how to undo what I'd said to them."

"Yeah, guess it's pretty hard to say, 'Guess what! I'm not dyslexic any more! I'm miraculously cured!!'" said Rachel, in her usual flip way.

Amber winced at her words, too mortified to care if they were taking the mick or meant to be mean.

It was a pretty awkward moment. Almost. Hurray for TJ for trying to lighten everything with a lame joke. . .

"Hey, there's *one* illness you've definitely got, Amber!"

"Um . . . what's that?" she asked, in a small, embarrassed voice.

"You're allergic to your family!"

We all laughed, nervously at first, but it somehow helped.

And I realized in a blinding flash that being the Cinderella of her family had really given Amber all the self-confidence of a slug, *that* was for sure.

I needed to say something else fast, to let her know it was OK; that we didn't want to make a big deal of what she'd done.

"Uh . . . how did you decide on all your so-called conditions, then?" I asked her.

"Well, that was the fun part," said Amber, allowing herself the tiniest of smiles. "There're all sorts of sites out there with amazing info, but there's plenty of nuts stuff too!"

"Like?" frowned TJ.

"Like this phobia website I found . . . it's just got some insane phobias in there!"

"Tell us, then!" I encouraged her, pleased to see some of the (pink-tinged) stress fading away.

"OK . . . got any idea what *Ichthyophobia* is?" Amber beamed at us.

"Nope," the three of us said, at around about the same time.

"Fear of fish," Amber explained.

"Huh? You're kidding!" we all sniggered, at around about the same time.

Amber went on to explain some more, like:

Hippopotomonstrosesquippedaliophobia: Fear of long words.

Kathisophobia: Fear of sitting down.

Lachanophobia: Fear of vegetables.

Pogonophobia: Fear of beards.

By the end of her list, me, TJ and Rachel were a) giggling stupidly, b) completely fascinated, and c) completely sure – even though we didn't say it to each other – that Amber was the newest member of Stella Etc.. . .

CHAPTER 18

Amberella *shall* go to the ball. . .

A familiar fat gull was swooping and dive-bombing somewhere down by the cliff edge. I could see it through the binoculars that we'd taken from Rachel's house.

If I didn't have a wedding to go to (sort of), I'd have wandered over that way. I was sure I'd find Mrs Sticky Toffee there, lobbing strawberry tarts in the air or whatever little sweet treat she'd brought along for the psycho seagull.

But like I say, I had a wedding to (sort of) go to, as well as a silly text to send right now.

"*Arachibutyrophobia*," I zapped off to Megan.

"*Dunno – fear of knees?*" she guessed back.

"*Nope: fear of peanut butter sticking to the roof of your mouth.*"

"Wow – bizarre. . ."

Me, TJ, Rachel were sitting on a bench in Pavilion Park, overlooking the closed-off gardens of the big house, where well-fed wedding guests were milling around the grounds in their finery like tubby peacocks. You had the feeling that any butterflies and bees in the vicinity would be drawn to the excess of nasty pastel colours going on, then promptly keel over from the deluge of posh perfume and aftershave.

Back at our bench, the only smells were of lavender from the nearby flowerbeds and Bob (an interesting fusion of mud and meaty chunks).

"Text Megan another one," TJ urged me. "Do that batty-wotsit one! I liked that!"

I checked the list in my notepad; Amber had told us so many excellently mad phobias that I'd decided I had to write them down so I could remember them.

"'*Batrachophobia*,'" I read out.

"Yep! Fear of frogs – excellent!" grinned TJ.

At the moment, I had a fear of everything still going horribly wrong for Amber, no matter what we'd tried to do for her. TJ was nervous too; he kept dropping the suede juggling balls he was tossing manically in the air. And the slight snappishness in Rachel's voice gave away a touch of tension too.

"TJ! Would you just put those balls do— Oh . . . *look* – there they are!"

Rachel was pointing in the direction of an open

French door, but we'd already spotted Amber and Si making their way down some grand steps on to the lawn. Si was saying something – something cheeky, going by the smirk on his face. Immediately, Amber put her hand to her mouth to cover the giggles.

"They look. . ." I mumbled, trying to find the right words.

"Like they go together?" Rachel suggested, smiling proudly.

"They look really cool, *that's* what they look," added TJ, approvingly. "Give's the binoculars, Stella."

You could tell TJ wouldn't mind copying a bit of Si Riley's style when he was older, though hopefully minus the lip-ring and black eyeliner. In his tight black suit, purple and black striped shirt, with a matching purple streak at the front of his hair, Si would easily pass as a rock star stumbling out of a hip MTV Awards ceremony.

"He did the streak in the bathroom last night," said Rachel, her eyes still glued to the two of them. "Got the colour all over the towels – Mum went *mad* at him."

"Check out the stares they're getting," I said, grinning as I noticed how many of the other

179

wedding guests were gazing over, their eyes drawn to Amber and her "date".

"They're going to be gossiping about them, of course," said Rachel, stating the obvious. "They'll all be muttering on about what they're wearing. . ."

"Yeah, and they're probably wishing they were thirty years younger and could be that cool too!" TJ pointed out.

All the women milling around, clones in their expensive, taste-free frocks and fluffy hats; they must have been gazing at Amber especially and wishing they could look that cute. 'Cause out of her badly fitting waitress uniform (and her baggy sweatshirt, *and* her lime-green carrot disaster), Amber really did look like she'd had a fairytale transformation, thanks to her personal fairy godmother, Rachel.

"She suits that skirt better than me," Rachel nodded over in Amber's direction. "And look at the length of her legs! They're as long as the M1 motorway. . ."

Y'know, if any TV producers were planning to do a teen makeover show, they should hire Rachel Riley as their stylist immediately. The flat black ballet-style pumps were Amber's (she'd run in them to Rachel's mum's shop), but the rest of her

180

outfit was pulled together from either Rachel or her mum's wardrobe. There was the tight, black, cap-sleeved T-shirt (Rachel's), the antique look bejewelled choker round Amber's long, white neck (Mrs Riley's), the flirty, flared lilac velvet skirt with the sweetest bow detail (Rachel's), and a tiny and delicately beaded black handbag (Mrs Riley's).

And as for Amber's hair, well, it hung like a copper waterfall now that it had been straightened. We were too far away to see it, but the tiny plait that Rachel had put in fell artfully at the side of Amber's face, a face that had had all the layers of gloop scrapped off it and replaced by a tinted moisturizer ("it'll tone down the blushing," Rachel had told her), a bit of lipgloss and sweep of dark grey shadow on her upper eyelids.

Instead of doing a passable impression of a drag queen, Amber now looked more like an off-duty ballerina on her way to present a statuette at the same MTV Awards show that Si the rock star was attending.

And the way Amber and Si were chatting and giggling together, it seemed like they were having a ball.

"Uh-oh – where's he going?" I fretted, as Si

turned and bounded back up the stairs and disappeared inside the building. "Give's the binoculars back, TJ. . ."

"Don't freak, Stell – bet he's just gone to the loo or something," said Rachel, reassuring me in her usual upfront way.

"But Amber's gone kind of fidgety, now she's been left alone. . ."

TJ was right – Amber's body language was now shouting out "HELP!" as she twisted one leg around the other, clasped her bag in both hands in front of her and fidgeted nervously with a bracelet round her wrist.

"Time for back up," muttered Rachel, hauling out her mobile.

"Have you got her phone number?" I asked.

"Yes – we swapped this morning at mine," said Rachel, pressing the speed-dial. "Well, I figured we should if she was going to hang out with us. I gave her yours too, and TJ's."

"Look – she's answering," I said, suddenly training the binoculars on Amber's hand as it dipped into the kooky little bag and pulled out a mobile.

And for the next couple of minutes, me and TJ became back seat drivers in this conversation, watching Amber (close up in my case) mouth *her*

side of it from the grounds of the big house, while Rachel stopped every so often to give us snatched updates.

"She says it's going great. . .

"Si keeps making her giggle by taking the mickey out of everyone there. . .

"Her mum's in a grump with her for running off like that, and the waste of money over the new dress. . .

"Amber doesn't care, 'cause her dad and her sisters say she looks gorgeous. . .

"Si says he's going to take her to a Buffy convention that's happening in the winter. . .

"And she says *no*, before any of you jump to conclusions, he's taking her as a *friend*. . .

"Oh, Stella – Amber wants a quick word. . ."

Rachel passed me her phone. It was strange to hear Amber's voice direct in my ear, but see her lips move through the lenses of the binoculars.

"Hey, had to tell you, Stella – there are lots of shopkeepers and town bigwigs here, and they're all talking about the Sponsor a Crystal Campaign. They're all up for donating to it – and knowing how much they all like showing off to each other, it won't be just a couple of quid here and there!"

My heart soared like a balloon seagull in the breeze – I was so proud of Mum for coming up with that idea.

"Great! I can't wait to tell my—"

The sentence was cut short, all because I'd just made out the letters on Amber's bracelet on the wrist that was tilted holding her phone to her ear. Black letters on white cubes, that plainly spelt out—

"Willow! Hey, Willow! There you go, one orange juice. . ." I heard Si say in the background of the call, as he lumbered into view through the binoculars.

"*What* did Si just call you?" I asked, though I'd heard it loud and clear, as well as reading it on her bracelet.

"Um, Willow," Amber answered, sounding shy. "He says I look just like the girl who plays her in Buffy."

"And you've got it round your wrist," I pointed out.

"Mmm," nodded Amber, glancing at the beads. "I sort of tried to give myself that nickname, but it felt a bit stupid. You know; having a nickname that only *I* use!"

I adjusted the binoculars so that my view of Amber and Si pulled back. Si was rolling his eyes

184

good-naturedly as she spoke, I could just make out. Closer to home, I felt TJ and Rachel's eyes boring questioningly at me, aware that something had me rattled. Meanwhile Amber seemed to be staring directly through the lenses of the binoculars at me.

"Hey, I saw the name 'Willow' written in dust on one of the windows of Joseph's house. . ." I told her. "Was that something to do with you too?"

"Wow – is it still there?" said Amber brightly. "I did that ages ago, one day when I was hanging out at the old place."

OK, so that part of the mystery was solved. But there was something else. . .

"And I got a letter last week. Did *you* put it in Rachel's bag? At the café?"

"Um, yes. I just wanted a way to say thank you for listening to me when we met up at the caravan park," said Amber, twirling her tiny braid nervously. "But I didn't know you very well then. So I panicked, and signed it as 'Willow'. Pretty dumb, huh?"

It was pretty dumb, but it was OK too. It meant that Mrs S-T was right about her and Peaches was right about her and all the spook signs were right about her – Amber was definitely destined to be our friend.

"Listen, Stella – I've got to go," Amber's voice cut into my thoughts. "My aunt is making a beeline for us and I don't want her interrogating Si and asking when we're getting *engaged* or something."

"Sure. . ."

Amber was waving her byes, and even Si gave us a "cheers" with one of the glasses before they wandered off, out of view, presumably to avoid Amber's aunt and snigger at a few more wedding guests.

"Is Amber 'Willow', then?" asked TJ, picking up the clues from the half of the conversation he'd heard.

"Yep," I nodded, lowering the binoculars.

"How come?" frowned Rachel.

"Listen, I've had enough of weddings," I said suddenly. "Anyone fancy going to the Hot Pepper Jelly? We can talk on the way there. . ."

"Yep. Let's go!" said TJ, sticking his thumb up at my café suggestion. Rachel seemed keen too, and was trying to stand up, only Bob had fallen asleep on her feet.

"Try saying 'teatime!' loudly; that should do it!" I laughed, putting a hand on the back of the bench to push myself up.

My fingers were expecting to feel old,

186

sun-worn wood, but instead, my thumb was touching something metal and cool.

"What's that, then?" TJ asked me, as I bent over for a closer look.

"It's an inscription. You know, one of those plaques people stick on park benches in memory of their granny or whatever," I told him. "This one says, *In memory of my grandfather. . ."*

Oh.

Oh, wow.

I stopped, too stunned to read any more of it aloud.

Rachel stared at me, then took up where I left off.

". . .*Joe Grainger, who loved to sit on this spot and gaze at the sea, and think of his faraway home.*"

"That's . . . that's *Joseph*, isn't it?" TJ said in a slightly squeaky voice.

There was only one word I could think of to say in reply: "Café."

When you're in shock, you should lie down – that's what Amber had said this morning. But stuff it, I needed a sugar hit fast. A really *big* sugar hit.

I'd thought this week was going to be dullsville, but it had been so full-on with weirdness that I needed a very *large* fudge sundae from the Hot Pepper Jelly to give me energy for the *next* batch of weirdness this freaky little town had in store for me. . .

From: Frankie
To: *stella*
Subject: Seriously nuts. . .

Hi Stella!

Did you get that cute Garfield card I sent you? Thought it looked a lot like Peaches – ginger, fat and crazy!

The money inside's from all of us (duh, like you wouldn't have *guessed* from all the girls signing the card!). Anyway, we all chipped in for that saving-the-big-chandelier-thing, or whatever it's called. It's not much, but maybe it'll buy a couple of lightbulbs for it or something. . .

Anyway, thought I'd let you know that after me telling them what's going on with you, Lauren says she's never coming to visit you 'cause Portbay sounds too seriously nuts. And maybe you remember, but Parminder has a phobia of pigeons, so she'd probably flip out if she set eyes on that jumbo psycho seagull of yours. Neisha's been going on to the others about being allergic to cats (she just invented that, like your mate Amber), but she told *me* that she's scared of ever meeting Peaches in case he reads her mind (and sees there's nothing in there – ha!).

Don't worry, Eleni still wants to come and see you sometime though – mainly 'cause she's got a long-distance crush on that Si guy you've been going on about. Can you sneak a photo of him for us to drool over? (Don't tell Seb I said that, or I could get fired as his girlfriend!)

Hope your room decorating is going OK, and don't let your dad paper over your brothers (it'll leave untidy bumps on the walls).

Miss you ☹, but M8s 4eva ☺!

Frankie xxx

PS In your next e-mail, tell me more about all those mad signs you keep seeing pinned up everywhere. And what's with that tutu-wearing goth girl Tilda? Is she for *real*? She sounds nuttier than a jar of peanut butter. . .

Out now:

A marvellous, mysterious, magical novel by
Karen McCombie

Marshmallow Magic and the Wild Rose Rouge

Here are some facts about Rose Rouge:

She's eighteen.

She's entirely fabulous.

She's my idol, my hero, a star.

She's fun (in a wild way) and wild (in a funny way).

She's a brilliant artist.

She dresses like she raided a fancy dress shop in the dark (yes, she's worse than me).

She collects jewellery with hearts on.

She smells like candyfloss and jasmine.

She lives in a grotty student flat in Edinburgh.

She's the best sister a girl could ever have.

She knows how to keep a secret – specially *my* secrets – better than anyone.

She's the only one who really understood and really tried to help during that whole, horrible time back in Edinburgh when—

"'Nother one?" asks Rose Rouge.

Me and Rose, we're walking through the woods that surround the old Craigandarroch Lodge, at the foot of the hill. Other ramblers have neat nylon rucksacks filled with water bottles and cling-film-wrapped sandwiches. My sister – in her scarlet velvet dress, black leggings and Doc Marten boots hand-painted with tiny flowers – is holding out a rustly bag of marshmallows to me. Her cheeks are bulging like a hamster's after a snack attack.

"Yeah, I'll have another one, if you've left me any!" I say, dipping the pointy stick I found on the ground into the bag and spearing myself a fluffy, puffy pink splodge of sweet gloop.

"One for you, fifteen for me! That's fair, isn't it, Lemmie? After all, I *am* the older sister!"

I love (and live for) the weekends that Rose Rouge comes to visit. She could tease me for the whole of the thirty-six hours she's here if she wanted to, I wouldn't mind. Pity she seems to be coming less and less often, but I guess she's got assignments and friends and a whole new life, same as me. But when Rose *does* show up – with wrists and hair jingling with jewellery – I keep her all to myself, too greedy for the shorter and shorter spells of time we spend together to even share her with my best friends.

"But *I'm* the youngest, so aren't you meant to look after *me*? Aren't you meant to spoil me rotten?" I tease back, watching my feet as I walk so no stray tree-roots trip me up. (I don't need another scab on my chin after yesterday's handstand disaster.)

"Don't I *always* look after you?" says Rose Rouge, stopping dead and pretending to be hurt. "Cross my hearts and hope to die?"

With her pinkie, she traces two tiny crosses over

the interlinked pair of hearts dangling from the silver chain around her neck.

It's a twin to mine; the Luckenbooth necklace she bought me for ever ago. ("One heart is mine, one heart is yours," she'd told me the first time she fastened it around my neck.)

"Yes, you *always* look out for me, Rose," I tell her, reaching over and poking my stick back into the marshmallow bag, in the hope of spearing another pink blob. "What you *don't* always do is tell me when you're coming home!"

"Yeah, yeah . . . but I know you like secrets and surprises. It's much more fun just to show up here and bug you, instead of giving you three weeks' notice!"

She's started walking again, tossing her waist-length tangles of tinkling hair back off her face.

I swear, if anyone caught a glimpse of her through the trees and heard those tiny bells jingling, they'd think the Queen of the Fairies was passing by. OK, the Queen of the Freaky Fairies maybe. . .

And who knows what any stray, sensible Saturday morning wood-strollers would think of me? I don't suppose it's every day that you see a (nearly) thirteen-year-old girl wandering through the Scots pines wearing a Hawaiian garland made out of genuine plastic flowers around her neck. But how could I *not* wear it, when it was a present from Rose

Rouge? (She always brings me presents when she comes; the cheaper and kitsch-er the better.)

"So, where were you last night? I wanted to talk to you," I tell her.

I'd wanted to spill the beans about my humiliating handstand. I'd wanted her to tell me how I could ever look Kyle in the eye again after that, but she hadn't got back to me.

"Last night?"

Rose Rouge scrunches up her nose as she thinks and *still* looks gorgeous. It's funny; me and her, we do look the same, sort of (big green eyes, snub noses, fat apple-y cheeks), but somehow Rose's combination looks amazing while mine looks stunningly nothing-to-go-wow-about.

"Yeah, last night," I prompt her. "You can think back that far, can't you? Don't tell me you're going senile already!"

"*Cheeky!*" she grins, lobbing a marshmallow at my head and missing. (Hope some woodland creature enjoys that later on.) "I just can't remember. . . Oh, hold on; yeah – *that's* right! Me and my friends were helping this guy in our class with his latest art project!"

Urgh . . . that suddenly reminds me that Ms McIver, our art teacher, set us an assignment that I'd tucked into a dusty, cobwebby, faraway corner of my mind and forgotten about. If she asked me about it in her class on Tuesday, I'd just have to say it was going to be a surprise (i.e. a surprise to *me* as well as *her*, since I hadn't a clue what to do).

"So what was your friend's project like?"

Hey, maybe I could get inspired.

"It's about the human body. We all had to wear these stupid costumes he got for us, then we covered each other in paint and chucked ourselves at this *huuuge* canvas!"

Hey, maybe I *wouldn't* be getting inspired after all.

"I was in a tutu, and I was blue – see?"

Rose grabs a handful of dreadlocks and shows me the evidence; blue paint in the tips of her hair that obviously didn't wash off in the shower.

"Mmm . . . looks kind of nice," I tell her. "But y'know, *I'm* a bit stuck over a project at school. Our teacher wants us to do some artwork for the entrance hall of the school, in time for the parents' night that is coming up. Got any ideas that don't involve me rolling in paint in a tutu or gorilla suit or something?"

Rose Rouge thinks for a second, then fires some suggestions my way.

"How about . . . a drawing of your school?"

"Too boring."

"A *model* of your school, made out of sardine cans, then?"

"Too complicated. And smelly."

"A self-portrait, carved out of a pumpkin?"

"Too silly."

"A self-portrait made out of marshmallows?"

"Too squashy. *And* silly."

"A collage of the Craigandarroch Lodge?"

"Too. . ."

I stop when I realize that the rest of that comment is ". . .perfect".

Rose Rouge takes my silence to be a good sign and carries on waffling.

"You could make the collage out of stuff you find right around here, Lemmie, like flowers and leaves and whatever. Bits of bark would be good for the tiles on the roof, and lichen would be great for the ivy creeping all over it!"

Craigandarroch Lodge is just there, in all its faded, boarded-up glory, the chinks of mica in the grey granite blocks making it shine and twinkle through the dark pines and darker rhododendron bushes. No one's lived in the place in fifty years, apart from whole dynasties of spiders and slugs and stuff. But from a distance – if you try not to notice the boards nailed across the windows – it still tries to look as fancy-pants grand as it once was, with its towering turrets and swirly-whirly curlicues. (That's posh for bendy bits of buildings, like wedding-cake icing, in case you were wondering.)

"Here!" says Rose Rouge, tipping out what's left in the rustly bag she's holding (three pink marshmallows, four white). "Let's start gathering stuff now!"

And so we do. Even though I don't know what I'll use them for yet, I gather up chunks of heather and bunches of clover, and dump them in the plastic bag. Rose Rouge comes back with bark and moss and the most beautiful coiled and unfurling ferns.

When the bag is full to bursting, me and Rose – bunches of ferns in our hands – go and stand on the waist-deep weed-fest that was once a long-ago perfectly mown lawn in front of the Lodge.

"Brilliant!" sighs Rose Rouge.

"Yeah, brilliant."

"This'll make such a good project, Lemmie!"

"Yeah, I know," I say, feeling like Rose Rouge's mini-me and not caring a bit.

A tiny someone in my head puts their hand up to remind me that I haven't spoken to Rose yet about Kyle. But it's funny, when I'm with Rose Rouge, nothing seems to matter as much as it did. . .

"Shh . . . is that a *deer*?" whispers Rose, whipping her head around to see a rustle of leaves that *might* have been a deer in the shadows of the woods at the other side of the looky-likey "lawn".

"Maybe," I tell her, though I'm not looking in the same direction.

Instead, I'm staring at the kaleidoscope of colour and shapes that make up Rose Rouge.

Now that all my bad memories and bad dreams are fading away – like they happened in a different life, to a different girl – I guess I don't need to rely on her so much any more. But there's one thing I couldn't bear to fade away, and that's Rose Rouge.

"Last one to the front door of the Lodge is a smelly kipper!" Rose Rouge calls out suddenly, grinning over her shoulder at me as she starts bounding over the wildflowers and grasses before I know it.

"Cheat!" I yell after her, all mumfy, maudlin thoughts pushed out of my mind as I race to catch up and prove that I'm no smelly kipper. . .